"Davis tugs at the ~~~~~~~~~~~~~~~~~~~~~~~~~~~~~~ y] sing.
Ulti~~~~~~~~~~~~~~~~~~~~~~~~~~~~~~~~~~~~~~
believe ~~~~~~~~~~~~~~~~~~~~~~~~~~~~~~~~
—*RT Book~~~~~~~ on The Best Revenge*
(4.5 stars, Top Pick)

"Davis has a rare, priceless understanding
of the human heart and the ability to
create lasting joy for her lucky readers."
—*RT Book Reviews*

"The name Justine Davis says it all. Nail-biting suspense,
blistering passion and simply grand romance."
—*RT Book Reviews*

### Praise for
### CINDY DEES

"Dees' exciting, action-packed story speeds along on all
cylinders, with a smoking-hot pair at the center of it all.
Your fingers will get exercise as they rapidly turn the
pages of this compulsively readable tale."
—*RT Book Reviews* on *Night Rescuer*
(4.5 stars, Top Pick)

"Two people tortured by the past find the strength to love
and connect in this romantic, exciting adventure…
A heartwarming story."
—*RT Book Reviews* on *The Longest Night*
(4.5 stars, Top Pick)

"Heart-pounding excitement and heart-racing passion,
making for a read you can't put down."
—*RT Book Reviews* on *The Medusa Proposition*

## JUSTINE DAVIS

lives on Puget Sound in Washington. Her interests outside of writing are sailing, doing needlework, horseback riding and driving her restored 1967 Corvette roadster—top down, of course.

Justine says that years ago, during her career in law enforcement, a young man she worked with encouraged her to try for a promotion to a position that was at the time occupied only by men. "I succeeded, became wrapped up in my new job, and that man moved away, never, I thought, to be heard from again. Ten years later he appeared out of the woods of Washington state, saying he'd never forgotten me and would I please marry him. With that history, how could I write anything but romance?"

## CINDY DEES

started flying airplanes while sitting in her dad's lap at the age of three and got a pilot's license before she got a driver's license. At age fifteen, she dropped out of high school and left the horse farm in Michigan where she grew up to attend the University of Michigan. After earning a degree in Russian and East European Studies, she joined the U.S. Air Force and became the youngest female pilot in its history. She flew supersonic jets, VIP airlift and the C-5 Galaxy, the world's largest airplane. During her military career, she traveled to forty countries on five continents, was detained by the KGB and East German secret police, got shot at, flew in the first Gulf War, and amassed a lifetime's worth of war stories. Her hobbies include medieval reenacting, professional Middle Eastern dancing, and Japanese gardening.

This RITA® Award-winning author's first book was published in 2002 and since then she has published more than twenty-five bestselling and award-winning novels. She loves to hear from readers and can be contacted at www.cindydees.com.

# DEADLY VALENTINE

# JUSTINE DAVIS

*Her Un-Valentine*

---

# CINDY DEES

*The February 14th Secret*

ROMANTIC
*SUSPENSE*

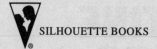

SILHOUETTE BOOKS

ISBN-13: 978-0-373-27715-5

Recycling programs for this product may not exist in your area.

DEADLY VALENTINE

Copyright © 2011 by Harlequin Books S.A.

The publisher acknowledges the copyright holders of the individual works as follows:

HER UN-VALENTINE
Copyright © 2011 by Janice Davis Smith

THE FEBRUARY 14TH SECRET
Copyright © 2011 by Cynthia Dees

This edition published by arrangement with Harlequin Books S.A.

For questions and comments about the quality of this book please contact us at Customer_eCare@Harlequin.ca.

Visit Silhouette Books at www.eHarlequin.com

**Printed in U.S.A.**

# CONTENTS

Dear Reader,

How sweet is love, but even sweeter if you snuggle up with this month's Silhouette Romantic Suspense titles (and as much chocolate as you can stand). First up, *New York Times* bestselling author Rachel Lee dazzles us with *No Ordinary Hero* (#1643), part of her popular miniseries Conard County: The Next Generation. Here, two lovers grapple with a mysterious presence in the house, uncovering a brutal force that could kill. Romance and suspense in one gripping package! *USA TODAY* bestselling and RITA® Award-winning author Marie Ferrarella sets our senses on fire when she throws together an unlikely pair in *In His Protective Custody* (#1644), revisiting her miniseries The Doctors Pulaski. A lovely doctor enlists the help of a gruff detective when her neighbor becomes violent. We all need a hero in times of distress.

You'll get double trouble and double love in *Deadly Valentine* (#1645), with stories from your favorites: Justine Davis ("Her Un-Valentine") and RITA® Award-winning Cindy Dees ("The February 14th Secret"). These authors present different tales of office romance, military themes, kidnapping—chock-full of passion, of course! Beth Cornelison continues her fabulous miniseries The Bancroft Brides with *The Prodigal Bride* (#1646), where best friends become lovers and maybe even…married? You'll love this roller-coaster read!

Happy Valentine's Day to you all.

Patience Smith

Senior Editor

# HER UN-VALENTINE

## Justine Davis

For the man who made every day Valentine's Day.
I miss you, ever and always.

# Chapter 1

"So what are you doing for Valentine's Day?"

Taylor Burke bit back the retort that immediately rose to her lips as she took the mail from the inquirer. If there was a holiday she liked less, she couldn't think of it. But that didn't mean she had to take the innocent mail carrier's head off when he asked a simple question.

"Working," she answered.

"You need to get a life, Taylor."

*This* is *my life,* she thought as she started to sort through the day's snail mail, so she could finish email, so she could get to her list of phone calls, a personnel problem and final prep for the big sales presentation.

Taylor reminded herself of that fact yet again later as she dealt with the second crisis of the day. She'd asked for, practically begged for this job. Three years later it was everything she'd wanted and many things she'd feared—mainly occasionally overwhelming.

But she shouldn't complain. She had responsibility she'd asked for, challenging work she loved, and a sweetheart of a boss who had given her a chance when anybody else would have said she was too young.

And "sweetheart" *was* an apt description of her energetic and clever boss, John Whitney, founder of Whitney Systems, lovingly known among his people as WhitSys. But lately the easygoing and kindly man she affectionately called J.W. except to others had been uncharacteristically tense and impatient. Something was bothering him, and she knew him well enough to see it, as if it hovered over him like a private, dark cloud.

Which in turn reminded her of her next unpleasant task of the day, due at any moment. She hated personnel problems, but it came with the territory she'd claimed as her own. And she would deal with it.

On that thought, Carrie Porter popped her head into Taylor's office. That Carrie was a friend made this both easier and more difficult.

"Happy day before Valentine's Day."

Carrie's voice was noticeably sour as she pulled the door closed behind her, which told Taylor she knew what was coming; that door was almost always open. It was the symbol of accessibility, and she wanted it that way. She was always accessible so that J.W. didn't have to be.

"I hate Valentine's Day," Taylor said, sounding almost as sour, and not simply in an effort to gain Carrie's cooperation.

Carrie blinked as she came in and sat down opposite Taylor's desk. "Shouldn't that be my line? I'm the one who just got unceremoniously dumped, via email yet."

"That's what you get in an office romance."

Carrie looked startled. "Wow. Cold."

"Maybe." Taylor sighed. "If I hadn't warned you about Will a dozen times I might have more sympathy."

*And if I didn't know you'd bounce to a new guy within a week anyway.*

Carrie shoved a lock of hair behind her ear. This week it was black with blue highlights. The woman considered her hair her form of personal expression, and had had the grace and humor to laugh when she'd found out about the regular office pool on what the next color combination would be. Taylor wondered if she even remembered herself what her natural color was.

"Okay, okay. I take back the early happy Valentine's Day."

"It's just stupid. What could be more fake than a forced declaration of love? Is that what people really want? Somebody buying them a frilly card and fattening chocolates only because they feel like they *have* to?" Taylor realized she was building up steam here and halted the flow with a flat, "I was wrong. I detest Valentine's Day."

"You're only saying that because you don't have anyone in your life. And haven't had for too long."

"Nor do you," Taylor pointed out, trying to ignore the fact that Carrie's cool—and factually true—assessment stung. There hadn't really been anyone in her life for a long time now. Not since she'd taken this job, in fact. And telling herself she liked it that way, that she didn't have time for a relationship anyway, didn't stop the occasional blast of loneliness.

"True, now. But I bet I could have by tomorrow. So could you, if you weren't so picky. You could reel in any guy you wanted, with that pixie blond hair and those eyes, but you won't even try."

"When do I have time?"

*You wanted this,* she reminded herself again silently.

"You're right," Carrie said, suddenly capitulating. "Valentine's Day sucks. Let's go get drunk tomorrow."

"Now there's a solution," Taylor said, knowing perfectly well this was another of Carrie's attempts to lure her out for a night of club-hopping. "And all the more reason to despise a holiday that can make people feel like they need to go get drunk."

"People in love like it."

*A place I've never been,* Taylor thought. *Not really.* "Good for them. I loathe it," she said with some finality, surprising even herself with her vehemence. When had she gone and turned bitter about it? Because that was how she sounded, even to herself.

"My, she's escalating," Carrie said dryly. Then she eyed Taylor thoughtfully. "You could always go after the new guy."

Taylor blinked, diverted from the moment of unpleasant self-realization. "The new guy? In distribution?"

An image of the awkward, almost bumbling man with the thick glasses, the every-which-way sandy hair and the unlikely name of Angus Kincaid popped into her mind. The guy had been there for about three weeks now, and was already annoying people. Including her. There was just something about him, his attitude, a certain tone of voice she could only categorize as whining. WhitSys was a great place to work, he should be happy to be here. She was biased, she knew, but it was also true.

And he was watching. Always watching. Enough

to make her wonder what was going on behind those heavy, dark-rimmed glasses.

Enough to make her nervous.

Carrie was grinning at her. "Yeah. The geek."

"Thanks," Taylor said.

"Hey, he likes you. He's always looking at you."

"Why does that make me feel creeped out instead of flattered?"

"Because he's such a geek?" Carrie suggested.

"Mr. Whitney hired him personally," Taylor said. "So that's all that really matters. Besides, he watches everyone, not just me."

And it was true. When Kincaid—he'd made it clear he preferred only his last name—first started his job, most had assumed because he had a nothing sort of job that he had a nothing sort of brain. But she had noticed the way he watched people, took it all in, and the fact that he never said much didn't make her think he had nothing to say. Just that he chose not to say it to them.

Then there was the accident. An inattentive driver had struck a pedestrian almost on their doorstep, just as she—and apparently Kincaid—were leaving. For at least fifteen seconds she had stood there in disbelieving shock, unable to process what had just happened before her eyes.

But not Kincaid. He had sprung into action instantly, long before Taylor had found her wits and moved to help. Fortunately, it had been more of a bump than real impact. He had helped the victim, a customer of Charlotte's Café on the lower level of their building, out of the traffic lane and was checking for injuries before she took her first step. Once the paramedics had arrived and taken over, Kincaid had vanished. And she'd had a question mark about him in the back of her mind ever since.

"So, is it true?" Taylor snapped back to the present at Carrie's question.

"Is what true?"

"That the guy's some dorky relation to the boss, and that's why he hired him? Because he couldn't get a job anywhere else?"

Taylor did know that the man had been out of work for some time before coming here. And she'd heard the jokes going around the office—it was hard not to—that the hapless and hopeless Kincaid was indeed a charity hire. But she hadn't—she would never—question J.W.'s reasons for doing it. Not after everything he'd done for her.

"I don't know," Taylor said honestly.

"There's actually something around here you don't know?" Carrie said in mock horror.

Taylor laughed, but knew it was time to take control of the conversation. "You've got to deal with your own situation before you start worrying about anybody else's. For your own sake, as well as the company's. You and Will have to work something out. We can't have two people who have to work together not speaking to each other."

"We speak."

"You blister," Taylor said dryly.

"Yeah, well…"

"I know you want to strangle him, and I know he's got it coming. But here, you have to work together."

Carrie sighed mightily, but gave in. "All right. I'll be good if he will." She eyed Taylor narrowly. "You *are* going to have this talk with him, too, aren't you?"

"Already have," Taylor said.

Carrie nodded as if she'd expected that. "That's what I like about you. You're fair."

"No, I'm not. I wasn't as nice to him."

And finally, Carrie laughed. Knowing her goal had been achieved, Taylor joined in.

"Just don't go after the geek yourself, okay? I don't need another office romance gone bad. Too much drama."

Carrie stood up. "Hey, boring girl. You could use a little drama in your life."

"No, thanks. I don't have the energy to spare."

For a moment after Carrie had gone, Taylor sat there rubbing at her forehead to release the tension. She shouldn't be so stressed, she told herself. She'd proved herself at WhitSys long ago, and on this job for nearly three years now, after all. And it hadn't been easy. People tended to look—or rather overlook—her petite self anyway, and the fact that she was blond, and her eyes an almost glowing sort of green didn't help any; they tended to stare at them and miss half of what she was saying.

The comm unit on her desk chirped happily. She looked down at the text message scrolling by. Tylr, nd u 4 shrt 1 pls.

She smiled in spite of herself. Her boss had invented this particular system to replace an office-wide intercom. He was much more comfortable with texting messages that needed quick responses than with talking into a box or picking up his phone. She didn't miss the noise of a standard system. She found the chirps—everyone in the office had their own distinctive pattern—rather amusing.

She didn't bother to answer, she would be there in less time than that would take. She hit the acknowledge button and got to her feet, grabbing her smartphone from its cradle just in case she needed to make notes. She walked to the door behind and to the right of her desk, which was also the side door to her boss's office. She hoped the promise that this would be short held true; she had a lot left on her plate yet today.

At her light tap, he called to her to come in. She pulled open the door and stepped into the sunny office. J.W. wasn't behind his big desk, but sitting on the small couch that faced the window to the west. They were on the seventh floor—the lucky floor, J.W. always joked—so he had a view of the mirrored building next door, and a slice of space between that let them glimpse the planes coming and going from the county airport three blocks away. The building was well built, and the roar of the jets was largely muffled to a faint sound most of them tuned out.

Surprisingly, he asked her to shut the door the moment she'd stepped inside his spacious but cluttered office. Her boss had a quick mind and a thousand interests, and it showed. Had he not been capable of turning some of those varied interests into practical, money-making products, she supposed he would have been dismissed as somewhat eccentric.

"I need you to do something for me, Taylor," he said, gesturing her to the chair opposite him.

"Of course." She sat down and waited.

"And I need you to do it and not ask any questions, or tell anyone anything about it."

Taylor's brow furrowed. *Confidentiality* was the watchword here at WhitSys. They were in a highly competitive field, and careless chatter could cost them. For J.W. to ask for discretion over and above the norm was unusual and unexpected.

But she knew one of the reasons he'd given her the job as his executive assistant was that he trusted her. She'd literally been the girl next door, growing up in the yellow house next to their tan house on the small cul de sac. She'd known John Whitney practically all her life, and his daughter had been her best friend before she'd been killed by a drunk driver at the age of fourteen.

Taylor's life had never been the same, but Heather's father had gone gray practically overnight. And had turned into the now fifty-three-year-old man who had channeled his grief into his work and ended up a bigger success than anyone would have ever believed.

She knew he'd give it all up in an instant to have his daughter back.

It wasn't something they dwelled on now, sixteen years later, but it made their relationship different than anyone else's in the office. He was demanding of everyone, which was accepted because he pushed himself harder than all of them, and because he was also eminently approachable and reasonable. But only from her—and his wife, Claire, who was like a second mother to Taylor—did he accept concern and gentle suggestions that he slow down a bit.

"I mean it, Taylor," he said now, his voice quiet and almost grim, another oddity. "This cannot leave this room."

She waited just long enough to show him she understood that whatever it was, this was different, special, before she nodded. "All right."

"I need you to compile a list of every employee who's left WhitSys, for any reason, and include those reasons."

Her first thought was that it would be a relatively short list; people were generally happy here. The pay was good, their work respected and their ideas listened to. Most departures were for other reasons, unrelated to any job dissatisfaction. And they were a small company, so that limited the number as well. But they had been in business for eighteen years, so if he wanted *everyone* who'd ever left—

"Taylor?"

"Sorry. I was just thinking that there aren't all that many, relatively speaking."

"I still need them all. Even the ones before your time."

She'd been seventeen when he'd taken her on as an intern. She had just finished her twelfth year, her third as his executive assistant, and had no desire to go elsewhere. She wasn't a tech head herself, but she loved being around it all, watching innovation happen. And she loved the challenge of helping him run this place, and the satisfaction of taking as much of the administrative load off her boss as she could, freeing him to do what he did best, innovate.

"The early records are on the old system," she said, thinking rapidly. "I'll have to pull the backups to search. That may take a bit of time."

"I need it as soon as you can get it. Everything else can wait."

The urgency was different, too. Unless he was hot on a new idea, he was usually more laid-back. She took her cue from that and stood up.

"I'll get on it immediately. You'll have it before I leave tonight."

"Thank you. It's nice to have someone I can wholeheartedly trust."

He sounded worried, and as she walked back into her

own office to get started on his request, she was thinking that had been a very odd thing for him to say.

She wondered why he would think there were people here he *couldn't* trust.

She wondered if he was right.

That thought unsettled her for the rest of the day.

## Chapter 2

"Hey, elf."

Taylor grimaced. *And here I forgot to wear my pointy ears,* she thought sourly. She knew her size, her slightly upturned nose, and her short haircut invited the comparisons, but that didn't mean she liked it. Especially on an already challenging morning. And from people she barely knew.

And, she admitted to herself, from people that made her uncomfortable. And the nerdy Angus Kincaid did exactly that.

Normally she would just avoid him, but when his cubicle was directly opposite her office, and she had to pass it every time she came or went, that was impossible. She was just in no mood this morning. It had nothing to do with the Valentine's Day; it had taken her until much later than she'd thought to compile that list of ex-employees. None of their current workstations liked the old software they'd once used, and she'd had to dig an old, discarded computer out of a back room and get it running in order to load the software and read the backups with the older personnel data.

Although the list had been short, with some names she knew—including one she had her own unpleasant memories about—and more she didn't, it had still been nearly nine o'clock when she'd finally finished. Oddly, J.W. had still been there himself; in the early days, he would stay until all hours, but for the past five years or so, he'd truly been trying to follow her and Claire's advice and ease up.

But no matter how he annoyed her, her weariness wasn't Kincaid's fault. Nor was it his fault she would likely have another late night to look forward to today; J.W. had the big meeting with several potential retailers scheduled, and while she wouldn't be present in the room, she would be in her office in case he needed anything. Then again, it was better than sitting home alone on the detested Valentine's Day.

She paused by Kincaid's cubicle, trying to think of a way to tell him to drop the nickname without coming off too harshly. He was new, after all, and she couldn't expect him to learn everyone's idiosyncrasies and preferences in less than a month.

"Taylor will do."

He'd jumped up when she stopped, but now looked sheepish as he stared down at his feet, clad in scuffed work boots beneath baggy khaki tan pants and a baggier, grotesquely garish Hawaiian shirt. The clothes seemed to go with a certain slackness of face and jaw, which had been one of the first things she'd noticed about him. All in all, it wasn't a pretty picture. The dress code was casual around here, but he'd tipped over into sloppy. Poor guy really was clueless.

"Sorry, Ms. Burke," he said, so apologetically she felt like an ogre. At least he seemed to be trying, getting here even before her most mornings. He just didn't seem to manage to turn that time into anything useful. And whined about doing it, which irritated her no end.

"Taylor," she repeated. "Ms. Burke only if you must. Just not elf."

"Oh."

With an effort, she reached for some of the tact that was usually closer to hand.

"You want to be called Kincaid, I don't want to be called elf. Seems a fair trade."

"Uh…yeah." He gave her a sideways look, or at least she thought he did; it was hard to tell through the thick lenses. "You don't like me much, do you?"

"What I'd like," she said, "is—" she stopped herself before she told him exactly what she thought of his job performance so far "—a large dose of caffeine," she finished wryly.

"You should try the Big Cup over on Front Street. They have a great caramel macchiato with enough espresso to wake you right up."

Her nose wrinkled. She'd never gone in for things that took longer to order than to drink. She was sure some of them were luscious, but she preferred to stick to simpler tastes and use the money she saved for other things. She got teased about it, but she stuck to her guns. And now she wondered how you afforded such extras if you'd been perennially out of work, as Kincaid purportedly had been.

"Thanks for the tip," she said neutrally, and hastened to get to the safety of her office. She definitely should have stopped for that coffee, she was clearly in a mood beyond snarky this morning. She didn't hate the guy, but something about him bugged her. Seriously. And it wasn't just his geeky exterior and slacker attitude.

She had her hand on her office doorknob when something she'd seen out of the corner of her eye belatedly registered on her not-yet-fully-awake brain.

She whirled back around and looked. But the paper she'd seen on his desk wasn't there, and Kincaid was industriously working at his keyboard. Or pretending to, unless he was the fastest typist known to mankind.

She walked back to his cubicle.

"What was that list you had?"

He didn't look up for a moment, as if she'd gone from worthy of deference to not mattering as much as whatever he was typing. His pace slowed, though. She stepped sideways to get a look at his monitor, to see what he'd been doing. She caught a glimpse of a program screen she didn't recognize before it was replaced with the company logo.

Hiding some computer game? she wondered. While J.W. was okay with a certain amount of that—they were a tech company, after all—Kincaid was hardly on the creative side of things.

"List?" he said when he finally looked up at her. Odd, she hadn't noticed until now his glasses were slightly tinted. Most who needed them wore antiglare styles, for the computers, but this was more. She could barely see that his eyes were blue.

"The page that was on your desk a moment ago," she said, wishing again she'd stopped for that hit of caffeine on her way in. She thought she had said it kindly enough, yet something flashed in his eyes and changed in his demeanor. She'd noticed it before, that quick instant of focused alertness that seemed at odds with the rest of him. But it was gone so quickly she thought she'd imagined it.

"Oh." The sheepish look again, this time accompanied with a nervous gesture she'd noticed before; he jammed his fingers into his hair and rumpled it even more. No wonder it looked like it had been cut with a weed trimmer.

"Sorry," he said again. "It's a list of people for a party I'm having. Am I in trouble? I know I shouldn't do that here, but my computer at home is screwed up, and—"

And again he managed to make her feel uncomfortable.

"You're in early. Not like it's company time. Yet."

"My...Mr. Whitney, he said I could. But I know you're the enforcer around here, so if you say no, then—"

"Never mind," she said, turning on her heel.

Boy, he was...something, she thought as she headed once more for her office. She wondered what a party he'd throw would be like. Would people come in costume, like the Goth bashes Carrie occasionally went in for? Dress as their favorite comic book or video game characters?

*At least they'd be out* at *a party, more than you can say,* she muttered inwardly.

She shut the door behind her, chastising herself for making assumptions based on appearance. Hadn't she just gotten upset with him for doing the same thing to her?

*Enforcer?*

Better than the Terminator, she supposed. With a sigh she dropped her purse on the desk and reached to boot up her terminal. She could only hope he would eventually be better at his job than he seemed now. Their distribution process needed some work, by somebody who could find and fix the glitches. And that section was one of her responsibilities, so she had a vested interest in seeing it running at top efficiency.

J.W. must have hired him for a reason, she told herself. It had to be her fault she couldn't see it.

And she was sure she'd just imagined that the paper on his desk had looked exactly like her very confidential list of former employees.

# Chapter 3

"May I ask you something, sir?" Taylor said as she added his last assignment to the priority list she kept on her smartphone. She'd already finished the biggest task on the list—putting together the individual presentation folders for the big meeting later this afternoon—so adding another wasn't a problem.

J.W. smiled, as he always did when she called him "sir."

"Sure, pixie."

She didn't grimace at that one. She didn't mind it at all from him. Because they had history. He'd pinned the teasing nickname on her long ago, when she'd been the never-still child who spent nearly as many days in his home as in her own. Since Heather had spent the other days in Taylor's home, it had worked out about even. He and her father had even put a gate in the backyard fence between their houses, they were back and forth so often.

He didn't use the old nickname often here in the workplace, only when she got formal with him, a subtle reminder of their long-shared and marred-by-tragedy history.

The memory of live-wire, bright-eyed Heather, the one who was going to be her best friend forever, tightened her throat. They had been as close as sisters, in fact in some ways much closer, and had promised to stay that way for life.

And in a way—a sad, awful sort of way—they had. For Heather's life, anyway.

Taylor gave herself a mental shake. "Sorry," she muttered.

"Don't be," John said, his voice so soft that she knew he realized exactly where her mind had gone. "It's important to me to know she's not forgotten."

"Never," Taylor said vehemently.

Heather had been Taylor's first experience with death, and the fact that it had been her best friend had made it all the more horrific to her fourteen-year-old mind.

"I was so young," she said, "I never realized until years after it happened how painful it must have been for you to be around me."

"It was," Heather's father admitted, "in the beginning."

"You must have hated that I was there and Heather wasn't."

"I can't deny Claire and I floundered for a while. But we never blamed you for being alive, Taylor. And it wasn't long before being around you was the only thing that gave us any peace at all."

They left it at that, both knowing that to go further would likely result in a breach in emotional walls that would disrupt the whole day. They reserved that for Heather's birthday, when her family and what was left of his gathered in her honor and shared the happiest memories they had of the lost girl. Just as happy, bright Heather would have liked.

"Now what did you want to ask?" John said, moving on before Taylor could.

"Angus Kincaid," she said.

"Oh." He looked, for him, ill at ease. Even wary. He seemed to hesitate before going on. "Problem?"

"Not really. It's taking him a while to get up to speed, but…"

She trailed off, not sure how to ask what she wanted, not sure if she should. But the memory of that piece of paper on his desk nagged at her. If it had been some list of his own, why had it had a note in green ink in one margin? The same green ink she used for notations, to differentiate from J.W.'s red?

"Not everybody can take off from the starting gate like you did, Taylor. You're one of a kind."

She was flattered by the compliment, but had the oddest feeling he'd said it to distract her from the subject of the new hire. It didn't sit well with the even odder feeling she had; he almost appeared guilty about something.

But she went along, for the moment. "I had the advantage of having practically grown up here."

"That, too." He smiled at her. "Smartest thing I ever did, taking you on as an intern all those years ago."

"Smartest thing I ever did was asking you to. I love working here, always have."

"It shows," Whitney said. "You're my good right hand, Taylor."

"Thank you. But about Kincaid..."

John sighed. And when he spoke, he didn't look happy about it. "He's...my nephew, Taylor."

She blinked. "He is?"

She thought of all of Heather's cousins she'd met at various times. She thought she'd met them all, but she certainly didn't remember an Angus Kincaid. A name like Angus would have stuck in her mind.

"He...he's on Claire's side."

She was sure of the guilty look now. Not an emotion she normally would ever associate with him. But he hadn't been acting normally for weeks, and now she was more worried than ever about him.

Brow furrowed, Taylor said, "I never met him. And Heather was always talking about her cousins. I don't remember her ever even mentioning him."

"He lived back east. Didn't visit when you were a kid."

"But he's here now."

"Yes." He sighed, took a breath and, still looking unhappy, went on in a rush. "He needed a fresh start. Had some trouble finding a job, and keeping it."

*Great,* Taylor thought. The office joke was true. He had been hired because he was a loser related to the boss. So much for the idea she'd had that there was something else, something sharper, something deeper behind his apparent geekhood. Apparently he really was just an office drone. And a not very efficient one at that.

"I need you to cut him some slack, Taylor, at least for a while."

She didn't protest, she wouldn't. "All right," she said simply.

He smiled, clearly relieved. "Just like that?"

"You're the boss." The relief faded, and Taylor hastened to soften the words she hadn't meant to sound like a criticism. "Maybe he'll get there. And besides, you gave me a chance when I was too young to know anything. I'm sure I was no prize when I started."

"You've always been a prize to me, Taylor. I'm not sure I, or Claire, or our marriage, would have made it after Heather if not for you."

They had long ago reached a comfortable peace with their place in each other's lives. Taylor could never replace Heather, they all knew that, but she still held a place for them, a special place no one else could fill. As they did for her.

"By the way," Whitney said, in the tone of one moving off a painful subject, "I need another favor. I know you've not been here since the beginning—it just seems that way." She smiled, and waited. "I need your best recollection about anybody who's still here who was also close friends with anyone on that list you made up for me."

Taylor's brow furrowed. "I'll try," she said, "But I don't know—"

He waved a hand at her. "I understand. But you'll have a better idea than I do. Just give it your best shot."

She thought a moment, gave him two names that came to her right away and promised to keep thinking about it.

He nodded. "And, Taylor? Same rules apply."

Meaning don't ask anything or say a word, she thought. "All right," she said, having more trouble at the moment with the no questions asked than the confidentiality. Keeping something a secret had never been a problem for her, but working in the dark was. Only her trust in her boss kept her from asking at least some of the many questions rattling around in her mind.

After lunch, she'd been back in her office less than an hour when a discreet tap on her office door pulled her out of the project chart she'd been working on.

"Taylor?"

"Come on in, Mark," she said.

The cheerfully brilliant young designer/programmer stepped into her office. That alone was an oddity; Mark Carstairs rarely came out of his large office in the opposite corner of the building. He spent his days there making J.W.'s ideas work, and he was a genius at it.

He also wasn't much for small talk.

"I don't mean to complain, but that new guy…" he began.

She just couldn't seem to get Kincaid out of her way today. "I know he's not up to speed yet—"

"It's not that. I mean, I know distribution's important, but it's not on my screen, you know?"

"Then what? Besides his general weirdness?"

Mark, who belied the stereotypes, being a fit, buff and sexy jock type who ran marathons for fun, shook his head.

"He's…always poking around. Interrupting. I can't concentrate when I'm wondering if he's going to butt in at any second."

She frowned. "He's actually coming into your space?" If there was a place at WhitSys more sacrosanct than Mark's domain, she didn't know what it was. J.W.

had always said he'd rather people interrupted him than Mark, and everyone here knew it. Especially now, when they were in the midst of final testing of Watchdog, their new, cutting-edge network security system. Mark was spending most of his days now trying to hack into a system protected by Watchdog, and so far the results had been promisingly negative.

"He sticks his nose in every day. Sometimes more than once."

"Why?"

"Dunno. Maybe he's just trying to be friendly, but he freaks me out. He's always looking around, poking into stuff while he's talking."

"Talking about what?"

"Same stuff he gets on to everybody. If I like working here. Don't they work me too hard, pay me too little. That kind of stuff."

Taylor blinked. "Do we?"

"What?"

"Work you too hard and pay you too little."

Mark laughed. "Are you kidding? With such cool toys to play with, it's hardly work at all."

"I'll talk to him," she promised.

And she would, although the thought made her groan inwardly. But Mark was a critical—perhaps the most critical—cog in the workings of WhitSys. He deserved to have his time and space respected. And it was her job to be sure that happened.

After he'd gone back to his domain, Taylor waited until an opportunity arose, when Kincaid was away from his cubicle. It didn't take long; he soon wandered off toward the elevator, perhaps to go get one of his fluffy coffee drinks. She watched him go, his hands stuffed in the pockets of those baggy pants, his lime green and pink shirt flapping around him.

She left her own office then, and made a circuit of the outer offices, stopping to chat with everyone who wasn't on the phone. She did this periodically anyway, as part of her campaign to keep everyone happy, so it shouldn't raise any eyebrows. Although she began to wish she'd held off until tomorrow, given the number of times people brought up or showed off flowers, candy and sappy Valentine cards. Even a couple of the guys had cards on their desks.

But during each chat, she worked the conversation around to the new guy. And got variations on the same theme each time. Kincaid was nosy. Or at least, had been; it seemed he had tapered off, perhaps sensing the lack of welcome.

Maybe he was just completely inept, socially, she thought. She recalled the first week he'd been here, a day when she'd given him a ride home. She'd been startled when he asked, and more so when he explained that he lived in the same general direction she did. How had he known that? Once they were in her car, she'd asked and he'd answered rather vaguely that someone had mentioned where she lived. And that was about the last question she'd asked, because the rest of the ride was filled with his questions about her.

Some had been the routine kind people asked to find out about somebody new, but some had been nosy and personal to the point of inappropriateness. What did it matter to him whether she owned her car or house, or how many hours a week she put in? By the time she'd dropped him off—at one of those coffee shops he said was near his apartment—she was thoroughly irritated,

and wondering what on earth J.W. had been thinking
when he hired the guy.

Now she knew.

She hoped those who said he'd backed off a bit were
right. Maybe he was just a slow learner.

When she had worked her way back to her office,
Kincaid was back at his desk, no fluffy drink in sight.
She told herself to knock it off. Because she didn't drink
the stuff didn't give her the right to snipe at those who
did.

"Give it a rest, Burke," she muttered under her breath,
wondering where this unlovely mood had come from
and wishing it would go back.

She pulled the door closed behind her, needing
the privacy as she pondered what approach to take.
And rather sourly wondering if it would do any good.
Perhaps being related to the boss made Kincaid feel like
he didn't have to produce, didn't have to do anything.
Except snoop into everybody's business.

*Don't they work you too hard...*

Or try to foment discontent, she thought.

She wondered if J.W. knew his hapless nephew
seemed to be looking for kindred souls, malcontents
who wanted to complain about their work. Or perhaps
about having to work at all. Had her generous boss been
sucked by family ties into hiring a slacking whiner who
could turn into a major problem for them?

She was frowning again, she realized as she walked
toward her desk. She had better get out of this mood
before the meeting. She had to greet all the visitors
with the deference due potentially large customers, any
one of whom could make a sizeable difference to their
bottom line this year. She would—

Her thought ended abruptly when she saw the large,

pink envelope lying atop her desk calendar. Her first name marched across it in handwriting she didn't recognize, bold, sharp lines with a decidedly energetic tilt.

Obviously a Valentine's Day card.

Almost warily she picked up the envelope. She was glad she'd shut her office door this time. She tugged the flap open, and pulled out the card inside. She'd meant to immediately open it and find out who had left it, but the card itself startled her. Because it wasn't a Valentine's Day card.

It was—in a clever, thankfully clean, and rather Dr. Seuss-like limerick—an Un-Valentine.

She found herself smiling.

*Exactly,* she thought as she read the verse again, the rhymed bemoaning of exactly what she'd told Carrie.

"Okay, points for that, whoever you are," she said aloud, and opened the card in a considerably brighter mood. And sat for a moment, staring in shock at the inscription in the same bold hand.

*Sorry. No more elf. A. Kincaid.*

She flipped the card closed, read the verse that so matched her sentiments again. Opened it, read the name again, still a bit in shock. How had he known? How had read her so accurately? It wasn't like she walked around advertising her dislike of the day. In fact, except for Carrie, she hadn't mentioned it at all this year, and she doubted Carrie would have passed that on to the new guy she clearly thought too geeky for her ubercool self.

Carrie. Who had been in her office just yesterday, while Taylor rattled on about her feelings about Valentine's Day. Had he somehow overheard?

She frowned. True, his cubicle was right outside,

but her door had been closed. The only way he could have heard was to loiter right outside, probably with an ear pressed to the door. Not something that would go unnoticed.

"Oh, please," she muttered aloud in the safety of her office. Now she was suspecting him of skulking outside closed doors with his ear pressed to the crack? Eavesdropping? Spying?

She nearly laughed at herself. She must be more tired even than she thought. She obviously wasn't thinking clearly. The guy might make her nervous, but he was probably nothing more than what he appeared to be, a family leech who felt entitled and was taking advantage.

Maybe the card was his way of trying to ingratiate himself with her, since she had the boss's ear. Although as a relative, wouldn't he, as well? And maybe that was what all the nosiness was about; he was looking for ways to curry favor without having to actually work.

She shook her head sharply. She was spending way too much time on this, and him. Resolutely she put the card back in the envelope and turned to toss it into her wastebasket. At the last second her hand veered and she dropped it on the credenza behind her instead; it *was* a clever card, expressed her sentiments nicely, and it wasn't the card's fault who had bought it.

And, Taylor told herself, just because he made her nervous, and she didn't like the way he had gotten his job or the way he was doing it, didn't make Angus Kincaid some kind of sneaky, dangerous character. That settled, she went back to work.

But she kept her door closed.

And tried not to wear herself out wondering if she should have told her boss about seeing what looked like that list on his nephew's desk.

# *Chapter 4*

Taylor finished up the final prep for the meeting, taking care to add on J.W.'s copy of his agenda her private notes for him. Her research had netted some useful information about the attendees, including that Mr. Perez from Perez-Benchley was an avid golfer and where he usually played; that Ms. Clarkson from Quick Solutions had been an accomplished equestrienne in her teens, trying out for and nearly making the Olympic team; and that Martek's Mr. Martin was a political junkie and not to let him get started or he'd hijack the meeting with his opinions. The list went on with pertinent facts on all the attendees.

Once she'd delivered it to her boss, she headed to the ladies' room to freshen up. She wasn't obsessive about her appearance, but neither did she want to greet their guests with her mascara flaking or spinach from her lunch salad in her teeth. She ran fingers through the short, fringed hair that required little else thanks to the skills of her longtime stylist. That was the main reason she kept it short despite the inevitable pixie, elf and other comparisons. That and the fact that her hair was very thick and longer styles looked huge and oddly disproportionate on her small frame. One last check in the mirror and she pronounced herself ready.

On her way back she stopped by the sales office, where they were bustling around getting their own presentations ready. Video, PowerPoint and a couple of old-fashioned charts on easels—Mr. Martin preferred them, she'd learned—they covered all the bases, and would do their usual stellar job, she was sure. Then she checked the table at the back of the meeting room, where Charlotte, from the café downstairs, was setting up coffee and snacks ranging from small sandwiches to tempting pastries.

"Looks great," she commented.

"Thanks, Taylor. And thanks again for having us in for this."

"We like buying local, and it doesn't get much more local than you," Taylor said with a grin.

Within the hour, Taylor was greeting and escorting and generally playing welcoming hostess. She didn't mind, saw it as part of her job to give the first impression of WhitSys. When everyone was settled and J.W. gave her the nod, she retreated back to her office, where she would stay until the meeting was over. And get a start on tomorrow's work, she thought.

The meeting went on, and on, until she thought she could just about take tomorrow off with what she'd accomplished. J.W. had already told her to. Usually after a late night she showed up at her regular time anyway, but this time, maybe she would just do exactly that.

Actually sleep in, maybe, and get a few things done at home. She could—

The sounds from the meeting room changed, and she heard movement. She instinctively glanced at the clock. After a moment, her boss opened the door from his office to hers. She stood up.

"How did it go?"

"Well," he said, sounding pleased, "Matt and Drew did a great job, as usual. You should have seen Jorge's face when the video got to how the side app could be used to track and analyze your golf scores."

Taylor grinned. "I knew that might come in handy."

"It did. I think it made the deal for Perez-Benchley." He handed her the papers in his hand, and she saw that they were indeed a sales contract. "The others are taking the data back to their bosses, but two have made verbal commitments right now."

"It did go well," Taylor exclaimed.

"And Martek still wants to hire you away."

"Not a chance," she said firmly.

Whitney smiled, but sounded serious when he added, "They're bigger, he could probably pay you more."

"You pay me just fine. And money isn't everything. I'm not going anywhere unless you throw me out."

"Not a chance," he echoed, making her smile in turn. "But I do need a favor. I hate to ask, it's already so late, but—"

"Don't worry. What is it?"

He nodded at the papers she now held. "There are a couple of fairly minor changes, mostly wording and dates, that need to be inserted before the final signing. Could you—"

"Consider it done. You want them on your desk?"

"A copy, yes, for the contracts office, but go ahead and email them to Perez-Benchley."

"It'll be done tonight."

"You're a treasure, pixie. And you take tomorrow off. I mean it, you've more than earned it. I'll muddle through without you somehow."

She smiled anew. "I just might," she promised. "But I'll definitely take you up on coming in late."

"You do that. You've more than earned it, and you so rarely take time away. I'm the one who should be lecturing you about working too much and too hard."

When she finally stepped out of her office an hour and a half later, the rest of the place was silent, the lights dimmed. Not even Mark, who often lost track of time when he was deep into a project and had to be reminded it was time to leave, was there.

And thankfully, the cubicle opposite her office door was long empty. She thought of the card she'd tucked into a side pocket of her purse. It *was* clever, she thought. And made her wonder anew if there was more to Kincaid than met the eye. Not that it mattered, as long as his intrusiveness with other employees had stopped. She would have had to deal with that, eventually. As for his lack of work, well, J.W. would only tolerate so much of that. Even for a relative.

At least, she hoped that was the case. She couldn't believe he'd really—

A tall shadow swept over her. Her heart jumped, pulse picking up as a man seemed to loom up out of nowhere.

"Working late again, Taylor?"

She took in a deep breath as Henry, the head of the night janitorial staff, turned to face her. She nearly laughed inwardly at herself; she'd never met a sweeter, less threatening man.

"So it seems, Henry. How are you? And how's that adorable granddaughter of yours? Any new pictures?"

The question would guarantee she'd be even later getting out of here—the man always had new pictures—but he was so proud of the newest addition to his large family she couldn't resist. She dutifully looked at the new display on the music player he used to get through the quiet nights. Taylor wasn't one who thought all babies were cute by definition, but this one was.

"Oh, you're going to have your hands full when she grows up," she said when the new batch had rotated through the slide show.

"Not sure we're going to allow that," Henry said with a grin as he slipped the device back into his pocket. "Now, when are you going to get yourself a good man and start a family of your own?"

Taylor laughed. It was a reflex, covering her wry thought that the likelihood of that happening was next to nil.

"You should be out with an adoring man tonight, not working late. It's Valentine's Day, girl."

"I'm running a little short on adoring men these days," she admitted glumly.

"One of these days," Henry said, "you're going to find one who isn't afraid of the brains behind that pretty face of yours."

"If you come across him, let me know," Taylor said, keeping it light to cover her surprise at the old man's perceptiveness. She knew she wasn't unattractive, but her appearance seemed to make people surprised to find out she was also smart.

As she waited for the elevator to the underground parking structure, Taylor found herself feeling wryly—or perhaps ruefully—glad she was living now and not in the age when a woman who hadn't done what Henry suggested—found a man and started her family—at thirty would have been considered an old maid. A spinster. Doomed to a life alone, obviously because of some huge flaw in her that made her unwantable, unlovable—

The faint ding and the doors sliding open stopped her thoughts. She stepped into the waiting elevator.

"Gee, no floor labeled 'self-pity,'" she chided herself aloud as she hit the button with the *G* beside it.

Her mood had to be brought on by Valentine's Day, she thought as she rode down the seven levels. It was messing her up. She didn't normally spend much time thinking about such things. Her life was full with work, family and friends, and she told herself that should be enough. Besides, her forays into serious dating nearly always ended in failure. It was more often because of her dedication to her job than, as Henry had said, that men were afraid of her brains.

She smiled as the words echoed in her mind. And she had to admit there was some truth to them, just as she had to hope it wasn't always the truth, because if it was she truly was doomed to a life alone, because she wasn't about to change herself, hide who she was—

The elevator chimed the announcement that they'd arrived at the subterranean garage. Just as well, she thought; she was getting far too esoteric for this late in the day.

She fished her keys out of her bag as the doors slid open. There were still a few cars scattered about, others who were working late, or some, she suspected, who simply stored vehicles here, since they rarely seemed to move. She heard a couple of people talking rather urgently off to the left, near her parking spot, then heard footsteps approaching from the other direction, heading toward the elevator she had just vacated. She recognized the attorney who worked for the firm on the floor above them, clearly in a hurry. She didn't pause to chat, just waved, and Taylor waved back at the woman who worked even more hours than she did.

Taylor walked toward her car, the compact crossover SUV that she'd bought last year when J.W. had given her yet another raise.

She pressed the button on her key twice and the little SUV obediently chirped twice in response as it opened all the doors. Whoever had been having that animated conversation was now nowhere in sight, although it was odd that she hadn't heard a car leave, or even a car door close.

She opened a back door and tossed in her jacket and the bag with a leftover sandwich she'd purloined from the snack tray, figuring it would save her having to fix something at home. She closed that door, then opened the driver's door and got in. She slid the key into the ignition and—

A shadow loomed up on the passenger side. For the second time that night her pulse leaped. And again she felt silly, when she realized it was the misfit, awkward Angus Kincaid. On the heels of that came doubt; it *was* Kincaid, wasn't it? But what would he be doing here now, and he looked so different—

Three things happened in rapid succession. Kincaid yanked open the passenger door and slid into the passenger seat. He slammed the door shut behind him. Then he turned to face her.

She nearly gasped aloud at the change in him; the glasses—those heavy, black-rimmed spectacles—were gone, and the difference from that alone was astounding. Even in the relatively dim and very yellow light of the underground garage she could see how blue his eyes really were. She wondered inanely if he'd worn the glasses for that very reason, to mask that vivid color, wondering if she should try that herself.

And then came the fourth thing that made everything else irrelevant. He moved so that she could see what he held in his right hand. Even in the low light of the garage it glinted, silver and deadly.

A gun.

Her first thought, stupidly, was that now she had a real reason to hate Valentine's Day.

# Chapter 5

In a deep, unruffled voice she'd never heard from him, Kincaid said, "Start it."

Taylor couldn't move. She just stared at the weapon he held, noticing inanely that his hand seemed rock-solid steady, and familiar with the task.

She finally, reluctantly shifted her gaze to his face. And was stunned all over again. The change was so obvious, so dramatic, that she felt the ridiculous urge to ask, "Who are you, and what have you done with the real Angus Kincaid?"

Or maybe this *was* the real Angus Kincaid.

The awkwardness, the geek-type demeanor, was completely gone. This was the same man, yet so different it didn't seem possible. It wasn't simply the clothes, and the fact that he now wore a pair of jeans that actually seemed to fit and a crew-neck sweater that made her wonder why she'd never noticed how broad his shoulders were. Nor was it that his thick hair looked normal now, if not neat then at least not rumpled in several different directions. It wasn't even the eyes, shocking though they were out from behind the glasses that had apparently been a mask of sorts.

It was as if he'd actually changed physically. There had been that certain slackness about him, now vanished. This was a man with a tight, alert look and a strong, masculine jaw. There was an intelligence that fairly snapped in his eyes, in contrast to the flat, almost dull expression that had been there before. The change was beyond startling.

The shambling movements had been replaced by a controlled, decisive manner that made her think of athletes or military types. Beneath the baggy clothes had been hidden a lean, rangy body that was too muscular to be skinny.

And she was insane to be sitting here like a fool, immobilized by the total change in him.

"Come on, Taylor, start the car."

His words confirmed her first observation; even his voice had changed. Significantly. Gone was the whiny undertone that had so annoyed her, and in its place was a cool, rough-timbred sound that made her shiver.

That unexpected response finally startled her out of her stunned state.

"You want the car, take it."

She moved as if to get out and leave it to him. He moved in turn, at first she thought to reach out and grab her, stop her, and her pulse leaped violently for the third time tonight.

But instead, he simply turned the key and started the car.

"If you're after money," she said, surprised her voice

wasn't shakier, "you're wasting your time. I don't have any that would make this worth it."

"Nobody else willing to pay for your safe return?" he asked, in a tone that was gently mocking.

"My family's not rich. If you somehow got the idea we have lots of money, you're wrong. We don't."

He seemed to study her for a moment. "But your boss does."

She blinked, startled into a normal reaction. "Mr. Whitney? What are you talking about?"

"I know how close you two are. It's kind of sweet, really, him hiring his dead daughter's best friend, years later."

No, there was no trace of the bumbling, awkward Angus Kincaid in this man. And he'd obviously learned a lot in his short tenure. Unless…this had been his plan all along.

"Are you talking about some kind of ransom? Holding me and demanding money from him?"

She should have been terrified, but she was suddenly furious. Maybe two scares in rapid succession was her limit. Or maybe just the idea of someone using the genuine love between her and John Whitney to steal money from him infuriated her beyond fear.

"He's your uncle!" she exclaimed in genuine outrage. "He gave you a job you can't even do, out of the goodness of his heart, and you pull something like this? You should be ashamed of yourself."

"Time was, I have been," he said, his voice taking on an oddly distant note. "But no more."

"If you need money that badly, ask him for an advance on your salary. He's done it before, for others."

"For you?"

"No," she said instantly, stung by the idea.

"A bit smug, are we? Because the brilliant, perfect Ms. Taylor Burke would never, ever get herself into any kind of trouble, money or otherwise?"

His assessment stung, and she resented it even more than she would have because it came from him, and she wasn't even sure why. She *was* careful, and she rarely did get into any kind of trouble. She didn't think—and wouldn't let him make her feel—that that was anything she need apologize for.

"Apparently I've gotten myself in trouble now, by not telling Mr. Whitney to fire your useless ass when I should have."

He blinked. Drew back. Stared at her as if a puppy he'd been poking at had suddenly morphed into a full-grown Rottweiler. A lopsided smile that seemed quite genuine slowly curved his mouth.

"She bites," he said, sounding impossibly pleased.

Belatedly, because like an idiot she was staring at his mouth, Taylor noticed that his entire expression, indeed his demeanor had changed yet again.

And she had the sudden thought that perhaps it wasn't money he was after at all.

Perhaps it was her.

The fear her anger had driven out flooded back in a rush that left her shaken. She fought not to show it.

"Well, now."

His voice was an almost gravelly whisper now, and again a shiver went through her. He looked at her differently, as if he'd somehow managed to read her thoughts, or knew exactly what possibility had just popped into her mind.

Or maybe he'd just noticed that she'd figured out his actual intent.

"Interesting," he said, almost musingly, "that rape wasn't your first thought."

"Your disguise was too good," she said, trying hard not to let him see how rattled she was now. "All that bumbling awkwardness, the glasses, the hair, the whole geek thing. Nice facade."

Because she had no doubts any longer that it indeed had been just that, a carefully crafted facade. She'd been right about him all along, that there was much more to him than met the eye.

She just hadn't expected his hidden traits to be dangerous. As difficult as it was to make the jump from the awkward geek to this man, she had to see him as he was. She couldn't deny what literally stared her in the face. For, above all else, her instincts clamored that this man was a threat, even without the weapon in his hand.

Which, she reminded herself, was still pointed at her. She should just shut up before she provoked him. Or maybe she should keep talking, try to reason with him. Or at least distract him, so she could try to get away. She should—

The car door behind her opened. For the third time in less than an hour her pulse jumped and adrenaline flooded her system. She barely had time to notice Kincaid didn't react—this was no surprise to him— before she instinctively jerked around to look.

And frowned.

"Arlen?"

"Whitney's favorite bitch. At last you're mine."

That hadn't changed. Arlen Sanders always taunted her for her refusal to go out with him, and for her disgust at his heavy-handed, crude passes. As if failing to see his charms meant automatically she was either cold or gay. It couldn't be simply that he, while admittedly good-looking, and capable of a certain surface charm, was one of the most undeservedly arrogant, smugly superior men she'd ever meant.

He was also the third name on that list of ex-employees. And one of two she had noted in that green ink as most likely to be disgruntled.

Apparently she'd been right.

"It's so good to see you again," Arlen said, in the same oozing sort of phony sincerity that had always made her skin crawl around him. But then he smiled, and unlike Kincaid's, which had seemed genuine, this was a malevolent sort of smile that made her shiver.

That shiver deepened when he said, almost gleefully, "And finally I'm going to get something I want from you."

# Chapter 6

Taylor kept her hands tightly clamped on the steering wheel as she drove. They'd be shaking if she didn't, and she'd be damned if she'd let either one of them see that.

Now that Arlen was here, he did all the talking, Kincaid had lapsed into silence. Did it mean Arlen was the one in charge? Was this his idea, and was Kincaid just…the muscle, as it were? He certainly seemed to have it; those baggy clothes had hidden a lot. Not that it mattered, when he had plenty of muscle in the form of that lethal-looking silver pistol.

"Think they could get away with taking all my hard work?" Arlen was demanding. "That I'd just go quietly while they stole it from me, got rich on it?"

Taylor tried to tune him out, but it was difficult with him sitting right behind her, spewing his outrage at perceived offenses with an unpleasant vehemence.

"Turn right on Alder," Kincaid said quietly, the first thing he'd said since Arlen had started his tirade. It shut the ranter up for a moment, and Taylor had the feeling Arlen had been completely unaware of where they actually were, so intent had be been on airing his grievances. But Kincaid had been paying attention. She wasn't sure what that told her, or if it would be of any use, but she filed it away to remember just in case.

*He's probably just heard it all before,* Taylor thought as she made the ordered turn. *Or he's just in it for the money, and couldn't care less what justification Arlen thinks he has.*

The question was, what was it that Arlen wanted? He'd spent this entire drive—five miles so far, she'd been watching the odometer—on this rant, and as yet hadn't said a word about what he was after from her, what he expected her to do.

She only then realized she no longer thought what he—or they—were after was her, specifically. Perhaps she was foolish to make that assumption or perhaps her mind couldn't deal with the idea. She knew that sometimes serial killers worked with weaker, easily dominated partners, but rapists? She didn't know. And didn't want to think about the possibility of them being both.

Besides, at the moment, despite the fact that Arlen was doing all the talking, she wasn't one hundred percent certain which of them would be the dominant partner. The Kincaid she'd known in the office, yeah, he would be the meek one, the manipulable one. The guy sitting next to her now? Not so much. Even without the gun.

"Can you cut to the chase?" Taylor said. "What exactly is it you want, Arlen?"

"I want what's coming to me."

*Oh, so do I,* she thought. *I want you to get exactly what's coming to you.*

A quiet sound came from Kincaid. She flicked a sideways glance at him, caught the barest hint of an upward quirk of his mouth before it vanished. Again, as if he'd read her thoughts and they had made him have to fight a smile.

"Left on Clover, then right at the dead end," he said, his now quiet, steady voice a stark contrast to the nasal tones of his partner.

"I want what's rightfully mine." The old whine that had once irritated her, as it had when Kincaid had affected it, crept into Arlen's voice. "I had the idea for it, conceptualized it and designed it."

She doubted he'd ever done that much or that thorough kind of work on anything while he'd been at WhitSys, but she kept her tone merely inquisitive, not wanting to set him off again.

"What 'it'?"

"Don't tell me you don't know about it. You know everything around that damned place."

She couldn't resist, she flicked a sideways glance at Kincaid. "Not everything, apparently."

Something very much like regret flashed in his eyes for an instant. At what they were doing? Or worse, at what they were going to do?

That thought rattled her, that what was coming could be worse than what was happening now.

"What is it you want, Arlen?" she asked for the third time.

"Watchdog, of course."

If she hadn't been driving she would have turned to gape at him. He thought Watchdog was *his* idea?

And that he'd had something to do with the design and implementation of it? A blistering retort to the absurdity of that rose to her lips, but she bit it back; it hardly seemed wise to launch on him while his cohort was sitting there with a gun trained on her.

She made the left turn, slowing down for the narrowness of the side street.

"You want Watchdog," she said, surprised she was able to keep her voice fairly level.

"It's mine."

"I see. And what will you do with it?"

She said it calmly, as if he were going to succeed, even as she vowed silently to do whatever it took to make sure he didn't. The idea of someone taking advantage of her boss's brilliance infuriated her. He'd kept Arlen on long after most bosses would have tossed him out on his ear, wanting to give him every chance to come around. And he'd given Kincaid a job just to help him out, and because he loved Claire. And now both ungrateful wretches were turning on him.

"I've already got a buyer."

"But it's not ready yet."

Arlen snorted inelegantly. "Whitney always did go overboard on the testing."

Which was why their systems were free of many of the bugs that plagued others, she thought. "So you've found someone not so insistent about quality control?"

"They'll get it to market right away, and make a killing. It'll end up a bargain for them."

"And what are they paying you for it?"

"That's none of your business. Let's just say it's going to make me rich. Like Whitney should have. And it will serve them right for firing me. *Me!*"

"It's always about you, isn't it?" she murmured, almost under her breath.

"And," Arlen added, his tone telling her he'd heard every word, "using you to get it is the bonus, Ms. High and Mighty Taylor Burke."

She saw the dead end Kincaid had mentioned coming up, and glanced at him. As before, he was watching her steadily, unwaveringly, the hand holding the weapon now resting on the inner armrest of his seat, but still aimed at her. He nodded his head slightly to the right, indicating the driveway to a small building that appeared to be vacant, judging by the completely empty parking lot and the large for-lease sign in a window. It wasn't until she'd negotiated the turn that she responded to Arlen's taunt.

"So it's payback, is that it? That's what all this is about?"

"It's about fairness."

"Spare me," Taylor said sourly. "If life were fair, leeches like you would—"

Arlen slapped her. She yelped. In surprise, not because it hurt particularly. Stung, yes, but the angle of attack from his position in the backseat made it impossible for him to get any strength behind the blow. Not that he had that much to begin with; he'd always been a soft sort.

Unlike Kincaid, now…

She shook her head. She had to be focusing on the amazing transformation because anything else was too frightening. It was easier to be amazed than terrified. Odd how the mind handles a crisis.

*Odd how your mind has shut off,* she told herself sharply. *Think about something helpful.*

How she'd ended up in the middle of Arlen Sanders's

revenge plot didn't really matter. It was obvious he'd gone well over the edge. The question was what to do.

As she parked the car where Kincaid pointed—he was suddenly a man of very few words—her mind finally began to function again.

Option one was to simply go along and pray they would let her go when—if—they got what they wanted. J.W. cared a great deal for her, she knew that, but would he give up the project WhitSys had devoted most of its resources to for the past three years?

The answer came to her clearly and indisputably—of course he would. She could end up costing this man who was like a father to her his crowning achievement, the product of his own brilliance and hard work.

That was not going to happen, she thought as they hustled her out of the car and over to what appeared to be a side door of the vacant building.

Option one was out. Because she couldn't do it. She simply couldn't do it. If Arlen were some unknown quantity, some stranger, and she didn't know how far he would go, then maybe. But he wasn't. She knew exactly what he was, and now she knew he was a coward to boot.

Kincaid was the wild card. He'd fooled her, and others, including his uncle. He'd hidden this cool, quiet and apparently competent man beneath a demeanor that had made them all either chuckle or shake their heads in wry irritation. But would he go so far as to physically hurt her?

She didn't know. But option one was still unacceptable.

Option two was to play at option one and try to lull them, then try to get away. The problem was that it would take time to accomplish, and she didn't want to think about being here that long. No one would even miss her for some time; she'd bet if she didn't show up at all tomorrow, it would just be assumed she'd taken the day off J.W. had told her to take. Her mom would call, but just figure she'd missed her and try again the next day. Same with friends, it would take time for them to realize they hadn't been able to reach her.

A vision of hours spent trying to convince them she was harmless and then escaping when their backs were turned was appealing and appalling by turns.

Option three was to just go with her gut and become such a nuisance they couldn't wait to get away from her. She liked that one. But Arlen had already slapped her, and it might not take much to prod him into worse. Maybe she should just test that water…

And what? Trust that Kincaid wouldn't use that gun?

She told herself to just get a grip and put it all on hold; it would be foolish to decide on a course of action before she saw what she was dealing with in the way of surroundings.

That Arlen had a key to the building was curious, but not particularly useful. He flipped on a light. Obviously there was still power to the small office building. And while there was no sign of any current occupancy, it was quite clean. She could even smell the faint, lingering scent of cleaning materials. Nor were there any broken windows to indicate it was abandoned, or had stood long empty. In fact, it looked ready to be occupied, cubicles and desks merely awaiting workers, as if the former tenants had just moved out and the new ones hadn't moved in yet.

Arlen had his hand on her left arm, gripping tightly

enough to be painful. By contrast, Kincaid held her right arm firmly but not hard enough to hurt. She noted the difference, but tried not to read anything into it. And now that she'd seen him dressed...well, normally, she had no doubts he possessed more strength than she ever would have guessed.

They passed through a waiting area furnished with a large couch and some end tables and chairs, and on into a spacious corner office Arlen had to unlock with a second key. As close as he would ever get to the boss's office, she guessed. It was equipped with file cabinets, bookcases and couple of chairs opposite a big desk that held a laptop computer. It was connected by an ethernet cable to a jack on the wall, she noticed, so obviously some sort of internet access must also still be working.

Arlen shut the door behind them. Once it was closed, Kincaid let go of her, while Arlen forced her toward one of the chairs.

"Sit," he ordered.

*Begin as you mean to go on,* Taylor thought, remembering her grandfather's advice, given to her once when she'd been anxious about starting at a new school. She remained standing.

"I said sit down," Arlen said.

She thought of telling him to go to hell, but put the idea on hold. Baby steps, she told herself.

"I do not take orders from you," she said instead.

Arlen's face flushed red. "You haven't changed a bit."

"Nor have you. Always wanting credit for things you didn't do. Thinking you've earned something or deserve something when you've earned nothing and deserve exactly what you got."

Arlen made an inarticulate sound that she supposed was born of fury, but managed only to sound frustrated. But he reached out and shoved her into the chair. Kincaid never moved. He merely watched, but in a way that made her curious. It was almost thoughtful. Or assessing. As if he were—

Arlen's snarl interrupted her errant thoughts. "You're nothing but Whitney's lapdog, you little—"

"John Whitney is worth a million of you. More."

"Shut up."

She ignored that order, too. "And he—and I—know how little you had to do with Watchdog. *Everybody* knows you were more hindrance than help. Mr. Whitney put up with more incompetence and laziness from you—"

This time it wasn't just an ineffectual slap, but a backhand with the force of a full swing. It was a moment before the shocking, sharp pain in her cheek receded enough for her to recognize the taste of blood in her mouth. And in that moment Angus Kincaid moved, and from the corner of her eye she saw him lift the gun.

She'd pushed too far, she thought. She closed her eyes, and waited for the shot.

# Chapter 7

Taylor realized how scared she was when, after the expected shot didn't come, she kept her eyes closed, with the crazy idea that if she opened them she'd see that bullet headed straight at her.

*What you're afraid of doesn't go away simply because you refuse to acknowledge it's there,* she told herself sternly.

She opened her eyes. Just in time to see Kincaid urging Arlen to sit in the big, executive chair behind the desk.

"There's a better way," he was saying to his angry partner, his tone soothing. "Just relax."

"She needs to be taught a lesson."

Kincaid straightened, half turned to look at her. "Sure. But no need to mess up that pretty face."

That "Go to hell" rose up in her throat again, but again she choked it back. This was the guy with the gun, after all. He had put himself between her and the enraged Arlen, no doubt saving her from another blow. She wasn't sure why, but until she knew more, she'd better keep quiet. Instead she lowered her eyes meekly, despite the anger seething inside. An anger that was only stoked by the lingering pain in her cheek.

"See," Kincaid said to Arlen placatingly, "she can be reasonable."

"She's going to be more than that."

"She will." Kincaid leaned in toward the man in the chair and lowered his voice. But not so low that Taylor couldn't hear. "But more flies with honey and all that."

Arlen snorted again. But he, too, followed Kincaid's lead and lowered his voice to about the same level, just above a whisper, as if trusting Kincaid's judgment about how far she could overhear. They were both wrong; she could hear every word.

"What? You think you're going to charm her into helping?"

"Stranger things have happened."

Arlen laughed then. It would have made her shiver with distaste if she hadn't been thinking so hard, trying to discern if Kincaid was just a lousy judge of how far lowered voices carried, or it was something else. The other option seemed implausible, that he didn't care if she overheard.

Then a third possibility, even more implausible, hit her.

He'd *wanted* her to overhear.

She was assessing that, turning it over in her racing mind, when Arlen's next words, slightly louder this time, came.

"The ice queen? Good luck with that."

He was sneering now. And his seemingly unassailable assumption that any woman not suffering from some kind of repression or disorder would of course fall at his feet infuriated her now as much as it had the first time he'd suggested they hook up for some fast, unentangled sex. He'd been literally stunned when she'd reacted as if he were an insane and repulsive creature that she'd found hiding under a slimy rock.

Which pretty much summed up her feelings about him from then on.

Kincaid whispered something she truly couldn't hear to Arlen, then shoved the weapon into his waistband at the small of his back.

"Why don't you give me that?" Arlen suggested.

Taylor's heart nearly stopped at the thought of this man, with his anger and craziness, armed with a gun. Kincaid at least seemed in control. Arlen would likely shoot her the next time she said anything he didn't like, which would be the next time she opened her mouth. Because there was absolutely no way she would help him steal Watchdog.

"This is my personal weapon," Kincaid said. "No one handles it but me."

Although she wasn't sure how she felt about someone who had a personal relationship with a handgun, Taylor couldn't deny the relief that flooded her.

A relief that vanished when Kincaid turned to face her. The expression in his eyes rattled her even more.

"You'll never get anywhere," Arlen promised him. "She's cute, but not worth the effort to thaw her out."

She looked away, toward Arlen, needing to escape Kincaid's intense gaze. And once she saw his smug certainty, she couldn't help speaking, even knowing it could land her in even more trouble.

"Some people just don't have a big enough blow-torch."

Arlen called her the foulest name yet and surged to his feet. Her glance flicked back to Kincaid, who was still facing her, his back to his furious partner.

He was grinning. "Nice shot," he whispered, and this time it was so low that she knew there was no way Arlen could hear him.

It was all Taylor could do not to stare at him in shock. Not just because of what he'd said and how he'd said it—proving that interpretation one wasn't applicable, the man knew exactly how well voices carried—but because the grin changed his entire demeanor. It turned his face from forbidding to charming, his eyes from icy cool to inviting.

And blasted any lingering images of the bumbling, fumbling Angus Kincaid out of her head.

"You shouldn't have to deal with her, Arlen," he said smoothly, easily, in a tone of male understanding of the difficulties of dealing with a difficult woman. "Let me handle this for you."

A sudden image born of cop shows and movies hit her. *Good cop, bad cop,* she thought. Was that the game? Was that why he'd interfered, stopped Arlen from hitting her again? Was that why the startlingly unexpected quip about her insult to his partner? Was he trying to lull her into thinking she had a friend, that she'd be better off cooperating with him because he'd stand between her and the crazy guy?

And if so, did he really think she'd fall for the abrupt switch? This was still the guy who'd slid into her car with a gun. Who had obviously plotted all this with Arlen. Who had betrayed his generous uncle.

He crouched beside her chair, his back still to his partner, and looked up at her.

"It's not what you think," he whispered.

"What I think," she said, not bothering to lower her own voice, which made him wince, "is that you're a fool, and a—"

"Told you she was a total bitch," Arlen said.

It was the note of satisfaction in his voice that sparked a realization in Taylor. He was pleased about something.

Her mind raced. Pleased about what?

*Told you she was a total bitch.*

Pleased about…being proven right? Did he think she'd shown herself to be just what he said she was, by her reaction to Kincaid?

*The ice queen? Good luck with that.*

She remembered the way Arlen had spread that epithet around the office. He had tried to get everyone to adopt it behind her back, after she'd turned him down flat for the third time and told him he'd regret it if he persisted. When he'd finally been fired, he'd screamed to the rooftop that she'd been responsible, although in fact she'd never told J.W. about it. He'd threatened to sue for wrongful termination, but it had never come to anything. She had thought that when he'd cooled down he must have realized he didn't have a leg to stand on.

Now she thought he'd probably just started planning his revenge. Or perhaps it had taken a while to build in his obviously twisted mind until this plan had taken hold. Whatever it was, she'd be damned if she'd let him win.

For that matter, she'd be damned if she'd let him take a moment's satisfaction in any of this.

So if thinking she was proving him right to Kincaid

gave him that, then she was just going to have to shove that satisfaction right back down his slimy throat.

"You're a fool," she repeated to Kincaid, who had been watching her intently, as if he were seeing her racing thoughts, "because all you had to do was ask, if you were interested."

Kincaid blinked. "What?"

"Did I tell you how much I liked my Valentine's card?" she asked, purposely making her voice as syrupy as she could manage.

"I…no, you didn't." He appeared puzzled, as if he were trying to figure out what she was up to.

"Valentine's card!" Arlen snapped. "What the hell is she talking about?"

"He gave me the most perfect card," Taylor said, in what she hoped was a fair imitation of gushing. "Made me look at him in an entirely new way."

That, at least, was the absolute truth.

"And I never had the chance to thank him before you did this," she said, allowing regret and distress to flow into her voice.

Kincaid stared at her in a way that nearly made her wish she hadn't said anything. She'd never felt a gaze so intense before, as if he were trying to look past her quickly thrown together facade of attracted female.

And looking at those eyes of his, she wouldn't be in the least surprised if he could indeed do just that.

*Diversion,* she thought. She needed a diversion. Quickly. She leaned toward him as he was crouched beside her chair.

"So, thank you," she said quietly.

And kissed him.

She'd intended it to be just that, a diversion, a distraction and a fierce jab at Arlen's bloated ego. And judging by the foul word she heard him spit out, it succeeded. Only then did she rethink the wisdom of prodding a man she'd already decided was unhinged.

But she hadn't intended what happened next at all. She hadn't thought much beyond her initial move, hadn't thought of what he might do in turn.

She'd intended it to be a short brushing of lips. Just enough to toast Arlen a bit. Hadn't thought Kincaid might kiss her back. But he did. He was.

It had taken him a split second, an instant when he'd been apparently too startled to respond. But then, before she could pull back as she'd intended, he'd grabbed the back of her head and pulled her closer. And his mouth had gone warm, flexible, almost welcoming against hers.

Some part of her mind screamed at her to pull back, to break the contact. But she didn't. And telling herself she didn't because she didn't want to find out he wouldn't let her go, that he would force her with that strong, steady hand, wasn't helping much.

*Unintended consequences.*

The phrase shot through a mind that seemed to be spinning out of control. And it fit, shockingly. Because while she'd intended to distract them, intended for Arlen to be pissed off, intended to throw Kincaid off his stride, what she hadn't intended was that he would kiss her back at all, let alone so fiercely, insistently—hotly.

But all of that paled beside the biggest unintended consequence of all.

She had never intended to *like* it.

# Chapter 8

She'd been wrong. Kincaid wasn't the fool.

She was.

It was psychological. It had to be. It was the only explanation. It was some sort of fear reaction to her situation and the shock.

Her reasoning sounded good, but didn't help much. Because she couldn't deny the sensations tumbling through her, and the incredible heat building inside her at the gentle but insistent pressure and probing of Kincaid's killer kiss.

*Oh, God—alliteration,* she thought with the tiny part of her mind that was still functioning.

But the fact remained that she hadn't responded to a man like this in a very long time. If ever. And she wasn't sure what it said about her that she responded now. Except that her track record of falling for jerks appeared to be safely intact.

Before she even had a chance to deny that to herself, a loud crash accomplished what she had been unable to—it broke them apart. The chair, tipping over as Arlen leaped to his feet in obvious fury. Her hesitation about prodding the beast had been wiser than she'd known.

"You bitch!"

This time it was shouted at the top of his lungs. He repeated it for good measure, adding an obscene modifier. And then he was moving, coming at her, his face mottled with rage, his hands fisted.

Kincaid stood up. In the action of turning to face Arlen, he moved to one side. Intentional? She had no idea. It was only a few inches, but enough to yet again put himself between her and Arlen, who was already raising a hand she was sure was intended to deliver a blow that would dwarf the earlier slap.

"Easy, Arlen."

Kincaid's voice was low, with an odd gruffness. Surely, her imagination, fueled by fear, gave her the impression there was a threat somewhere beneath the quiet words. A threat not aimed at her, but at his partner in crime.

The spinning in her head didn't stop, merely shifted direction. It almost seemed as if he were trying to protect her, she thought.

Only then did she realize her fingers were at her mouth, touching her lips where his had been.

*Snap out of it,* she ordered herself. *It's all part of it. Good cop, bad cop, it's part of his plan. Maybe their plan, maybe they worked this all out ahead of time. Don't be a fool yourself and fall for it.*

"Come on, Arlen. You've planned this for so long, are you going to let her distract you from the goal?"

Amazingly, Arlen stopped in his tracks. His fists

were still clenched, but he was no longer barreling toward her.

"Don't let doing something stupid stop you from getting what's coming to you," Kincaid said.

Taylor's breath caught. Had he used those words intentionally? She'd had the feeling Kincaid had known exactly what she'd been thinking when Arlen had used them.

*Don't be an idiot,* she ordered herself. *He's using Arlen's own words for Arlen, not for my sake. He's not trying to…tell me anything.*

But he had, by accident or design, put himself in between them.

"You focus on the big prize," Kincaid was saying. "Let me keep working her."

The phrase made Taylor bristle. But she again held back; she couldn't deny her relief that, for the moment at least, Arlen appeared to be listening. At least, his fists were relaxing. The backhand had been bad enough, and her cheek still hurt. She didn't want to think what damage a fist could do.

And then Kincaid had his hand on her elbow, urging her to her feet. She hesitated, fearing she was playing into their hands, but she honestly did not want to spend another minute in the same room with the dangerous—to her at least—Arlen Sanders. So she stood up.

Kincaid then urged her toward the outer office. Arlen was instantly suspicious.

"What the hell are you doing?"

Kincaid gave the man a conspiratorial wink. "Little privacy, y'know?"

"Like hell. I want her—"

"I know," Kincaid interrupted, making the exchange a weird sort of double entendre.

"I'm not risking her getting away."

"She won't," Kincaid said, at the moment Taylor was silently promising herself if the chance arose, that was exactly what would happen.

Kincaid lowered his voice again, leaning toward Arlen, but again loud enough for her to hear. "Besides, there's a couch out there," he said, his voice sounding full of smug male.

Taylor was getting mightily tired of biting her tongue. She had no other choice except to go along. Arlen might be soft, yet she now knew Kincaid was anything but. And while she was quick, and relatively fit, any idea that she might be able to overpower him or surprise him had vanished once she'd seen the real Kincaid that had been so completely hidden behind the nerdy disguise.

"We'll leave the door open," Kincaid said. "And if this doesn't work, well, she's all yours."

Something flashed in Arlen's eyes then, something bright and quick and frightening. And it suddenly struck Taylor; he hadn't gone to any trouble at all to conceal himself. He'd kidnapped her, openly exposing himself, knowing she would know him instantly. So obviously he didn't care that she knew he was the one behind this, that he was the one who intended to pirate the Watchdog system and sell it, and didn't mind committing a major felony to do it.

Almost numbly she followed Kincaid's lead, glad of any distance between her and Arlen Sanders. Because there was only one reason she could think of that explained why he was being so open about this. Why he hadn't cared that she'd seen him, that she would know him.

He wasn't worried she would tell anyone afterward. And there was only one way he could guarantee that. He had to kill her.

# Chapter 9

Kincaid's hand on her arm was oddly steadying as they left the big inner office for the smaller reception office. He led her to the couch. She wanted to resist, but her realization of Arlen's probable intentions for her had shaken her to the core.

In a rush of emotion she thought of all the things she'd put off as she built her career, all the time she'd missed with her family, the way she'd not bothered to put much effort into looking for a serious relationship, or starting a family of her own, thinking she had plenty of time.

And now she might have no time left.

She sank down onto the couch, little shivers going through her, weakening her knees. Only then was she aware that Arlen was standing in the inner-office doorway, watching. That made her shiver even harder, and when Kincaid sat down beside her, she welcomed his warmth.

And there seemed to be a lot of it.

She was about to lean into him, vaguely aware that he smelled good, some spicy masculine scent. She caught herself as she started to move that way, caught herself as she turned to him for refuge.

"Well, now," he said, "that's better, elf."

The despised nickname snapped her back the way nothing else could have. She wanted to slap him, indeed her hand moved, but she stopped herself, barely. She didn't want to start anything now, when Arlen was right there within easy reach. While it would be difficult to get away from Kincaid, it would be impossible to get away from both of them together.

She should play along, and try to lull him, then make a break for it, she thought. And after the way she'd stupidly responded to his kiss in the other room, maybe it wouldn't be so hard to convince him she was enthralled. Because maybe she was, just a little.

Stockholm syndrome, wasn't that what they called it? After those hostages who had ended up defending the perpetrators of the terror? Any act of kindness, or even just lack of abuse, had the victims grateful to their captors, and ended in a perverse distortion of reality that had them siding with them.

Pinning her hopes on Kincaid, even though he had saved her from further damage at the hands of Arlen Sanders, was beyond foolish.

"Maybe I'll let you warm her up for me after all," Arlen drawled in that smug tone. "Kiss him again. I'll watch."

The order, and the idea of him watching her do anything, made her stomach roil.

"Good idea," Kincaid said, turning her face with a gentle but insistent pressure from his fingers. His voice was oddly rough, but she supposed it was all part of the act.

She pulled back instinctively. So much for going along with him.

"No?" Kincaid asked. "All right, then I'll do the work. I want another taste."

Before Taylor had time to do anything beyond register that he hadn't gotten angry at her refusal, his mouth was on hers. And then she couldn't seem to think at all. Not clearly anyway. When she should be plotting an escape, all she could do was feel his lips, warm, coaxing, tempting. When she should have been pulling away, the urge to lean into him was almost irresistible. When she should have fought him, hard, she couldn't seem to find the strength to protest.

The heat that flooded her seemed to sap away every bit of determination, every ounce of resolve she had. Her muscles seemed slack, useless for anything except... kissing him back. And, God help her, she was.

She called herself names full of words she'd never spoken before. Still, she kissed him back. Clung to him as he deepened the kiss, moving his mouth over hers, his tongue touching, tasting, probing. Gently, seemingly careful of the tender spot where her cheek and mouth still hurt, he buried her in sensations. He was surrounding her, swamping her, and she couldn't seem to stop her own body's hot, unexpected—and unwelcome—response.

Sick.

She had to be sick in some way, mentally sick. What else would explain the fact that the fiercest reaction she'd ever had to a kiss or for that matter to any man would come now, at the hands of a man who literally held her life in those hands?

It wasn't until she felt him shift, bearing down on her, that she realized he had pressed her down on the couch. If she were reacting sanely, she should feel trapped. Instead, her body welcomed the warm, taut weight of him. Savored it. Wanted more. So much more that no rationale of how long it had been since she'd really been with anyone, or of how scared she was, could explain it.

There was more at work here, and the only thing that made sense was what she'd thought of before, that hostage syndrome.

It wasn't just his mouth on hers, or his weight pressing her into the cushions of the couch. It was his hands, stroking, caressing, seeming to light more of those unexpected fires wherever he touched. And the fact that his breathing had deepened, quickened, as if he were responding as intensely as she was.

It was an act, she told herself desperately. Just an act, designed to seduce her into cooperating. Wasn't it?

His left hand cupped her breast, his thumb brushing, then rubbing at a nipple she only now realized was already taut and ready for his attention. Heat blasted through her anew, and she nearly gasped at the onslaught. She barely managed not to arch upward to him, silently begging for more.

"You going to do her right now?"

Arlen's words, spoken in a voice no longer angry, sounding merely curious—and slimily entertained— were the bucket of ice water she needed.

That, and the fact that Kincaid broke the kiss. She was disgusted with herself that she felt the loss of his mouth and had to suppress a tiny moan of protest.

And imagined that she felt a shiver of the same kind of protest went through him, a self-deluding fantasy that made her even more disgusted with herself.

"Back off, Arlen," Kincaid growled, his own voice husky and harsh. He was breathing quickly, and when she moved slightly under him he made an abrupt sound, as if that breath had caught in his throat. Belatedly she realized that at least some part of this was real, because he was fully, hotly aroused.

Arlen laughed. It was not a pleasant sound.

Taylor moved again, this time determined to regain her sanity. She would get free of him somehow. But he was so strong, so much stronger and tougher than she ever would have imagined.

"Hold still," he said, so quietly she knew Arlen couldn't have heard it, even though he was barely ten feet away.

"Get off me," she snapped.

"You weren't fighting him a minute ago," Arlen said, coming closer. And the change in his voice, as if he'd discovered a newfound pleasure in watching, made her skin crawl.

"You're not helping," Kincaid said sharply, throwing his partner a look over his shoulder. "I said back off. I'll get you what you want, just back off."

Taylor wasn't sure whether it was the promise or something in the look Kincaid gave him that convinced Arlen, but he backed up to stand in the doorway again. Apparently he was enjoying himself too much to leave altogether.

Or he didn't trust Kincaid.

*Don't even get to hoping that,* she ordered herself silently, as she tried to squirm out from under the now not-so-welcome but somehow still-tempting weight of the man pressing her down with his body. That lean, hard body that had been such a shock.

"Hold still," he repeated, again in that whisper, only this time there was a note of near pain in his voice as she bucked against his still-rigid arousal. "I'm trying to help."

"I'll just bet you are." She pushed against his chest with both hands. It was like trying to move a rock wall.

"Taylor, listen to me," he whispered, his mouth almost brushing her ear. His breath tickled the sensitive nerve endings, made her shiver.

She was such a fool. She'd responded like some love-starved, sex-hungry idiot female, when what she should have been doing was figuring a way out of this.

"I'm trying to help you," he whispered again.

She lowered her own voice this time, not wanting Arlen to know she'd guessed his plans. "Sure you are. Help me right into a grave?"

He went still.

"You think I don't know he plans to kill me?" It was hard to keep that one at a whisper.

"I'm not sure he's planned anything," Kincaid said, sounding nothing less than rueful. "That's what makes him so unpredictable."

"You're the one who decided do this with him."

"I didn't decide. I was hired."

Arlen was still there, watching, but not reacting; he must think Kincaid was plying her with sweet nothings whispered in her ear.

"So how much is he paying you to become a felon, a kidnapper?"

"That wasn't the plan, and he's not the one paying me."

That stopped her thoughts dead for a moment. There was someone else involved? Someone both Kincaid and Arlen were working for? Just how big was this operation, and who really was behind it?

She was unable to stop the question even though she doubted he'd answer.

"Who is?"

He lifted his head, stared down at her with an intensity she'd never seen before, as if he were trying to will her to listen and believe.

"John Whitney," he said.

# Chapter 10

Taylor stared up at her captor in shocked disbelief.

"What?" she finally managed to choke out, barely remembering in time to keep her voice to that whisper.

"You heard me. Your boss hired me."

She couldn't believe it. Wouldn't believe it.

"J.W. would never hurt me," she said, shaking her head.

For a moment Kincaid looked puzzled. Then he shook his head in turn. "Not this. Grabbing you, I mean. That idiocy was pure Sanders."

And then, startling her, he kissed her again. She stiffened, and he tightened his arms around her, using his weight to once more hold her in place.

"Appearances," he whispered against her ear, the teasing brush of his breath causing that annoying shiver again.

Under her breath she used one of those unaccustomed, foul words. And to her surprise, Kincaid chuckled nearly as quietly.

Then he laid a soft, impossibly sweet trail of kisses over her brow, along her cheek, down the side of her throat. Her own breath caught as his had, and she hated herself for it. She needed to focus, now perhaps more than ever in her life. Yet how could she when every kiss seemed to start its own little fire, and the string of them threatened to burst into a wall of flame and drive her mad?

"Listen," he whispered as he trailed back up to her ear again. "John knew something was going on. He brought me in to find out what. And who."

"Brought you in? Are you saying you're a cop or something?"

"Or something," he answered, nuzzling her neck.

*What,* she thought, *a private investigator?* WhitSys didn't have much in the way of physical security, it hadn't seemed necessary. Technical system security, yes, of course, that was a huge part of their business. So if J.W. had felt it necessary, he would have had to go outside for that kind of help.

"I discovered several employees had," Kincaid said, "unknown to each other, been approached in the past few weeks, by an anonymous contact from the outside, someone who was after inside help."

She went still. And only then did she realize that he had, with that clever, irresistible mouth, nudged her head to one side, toward the back of the couch, no doubt to further muffle their words. That mouth—how had she ever thought it sulky?

She answered her own question immediately. If he was telling her the truth—and she wasn't yet convinced—then she'd thought it sulky, and him terminally geeky, because that was exactly what he'd wanted her, and everyone else, to think.

This wasn't the time to deal with that. She needed to find out if he was telling the truth. And fast.

"Arlen?" she asked.

"Mmm-hmm." He shifted his body, drawing up one leg over her, effectively enveloping her. Trapped. Not that she hadn't been before, but now it was…

She couldn't dwell on what it was, or all the sensations rocketing through her. And yet he kept talking, as if he were feeling none of it.

As, perhaps, he wasn't.

Except…he was still aroused. Completely.

*Like any guy wouldn't be, the way she was reacting to him? You're the only fool in this operation,* she told herself sternly.

"So I set myself up as a likely prospect, a slacker relative who had little interest in really working. It was the perfect bait. And eventually word got around and Arlen bit."

"Birds of a feather," she said, forcing herself to think through the lovely haze wrapped around her.

"Exactly."

It all felt too damned real. The heavy breathing, the eager touching, the occasional quick, nearly silent gasp, it was an act, yet felt more real than anything she'd ever experienced.

She needed to—no, she *had* to focus, she told herself again. And she grasped at that only thing she could think of that would help.

"Why didn't you—or J.W.—tell me?"

He seemed to hesitate a moment, flicking his

tongue searingly over her collarbone before answering. Formulating a lie?

"We didn't know if he'd already recruited someone, someone we hadn't found out about yet."

With those damnably hot and arousing kisses continuing, it was all she could do to process what he'd said. When she did, she stiffened.

"Good," he said. "A little resistance plays well."

She ignored the admission that they were just playing parts; she'd deal with that—and herself—later. Right now it was a struggle to keep her voice to the necessary whisper. Righteous outrage wasn't a quiet emotion.

"You thought it was *me?*"

"Give it up, man," Arlen called from the doorway, cooling her outrage with a jolt of fear. "This won't work."

"Not with you hovering," Kincaid said sharply. "Back off, Arlen. Go make sure your computer's ready."

To her surprise, Arlen chuckled. It wasn't a pleasant sound, however. "I'll be right back," he promised. "Maybe you'll have some clothes off her by then."

Taylor shivered, but Kincaid merely picked up where he'd left off.

"John swore it couldn't be you," he said. "He said he'd trust you with his life."

That mollified her a bit. "But you didn't believe him."

He gave a half shrug as he smoothed an errant strand of her hair back from her face, then kissed the spot he'd bared. She reacted in spite of herself, wishing he wasn't quite so good at this, almost wishing the awkward, bumbling Kincaid would reappear.

"He's a good man. A decent, honest man. They're sometimes the easiest to fool."

She supposed he was right, and her anger cooled a little. J.W. was a decent, honest man, and he thought the same of others. Sort of a corollary to her grandfather's old saying, "You don't look under the bed unless you've hidden there yourself," she thought. If you never have or would, you don't assume others are, either.

"And you have complete access. And knowledge. That's one of the first things I learned at WhitSys, that if anyone wanted to know anything, or needed anything done, Taylor Burke was the go-to."

She wondered if he was trying to flatter her. If this was all some story concocted to win her trust, all part of the plan to gain her cooperation.

"You have to see you were a likely suspect."

An almost pleading note had come into his voice, as if it were important beyond this moment that she understand.

"It makes sense, yes," she admitted. If his claims were true, then from his outside perspective, not knowing the depth of the connection between she and her boss, she was indeed a likely possibility for Arlen's mole.

He seemed relieved at her answer. As if it had mattered to him that she not be angry.

*Because then I won't cooperate?*

She wasn't sure she believed any of this, despite the ring of truth. But she also knew her perceptions were foggy, stirred up by his touches, his kisses, and turned inside out by the fact that his voice had taken on a rough, husky note that was just enough to make her wonder how cool and calculating he actually was.

"A little cooperation now wouldn't be amiss," he whispered against her ear.

That he echoed her own thoughts made her suspicious all over again.

"If you think I'm going to march in there and download Watchdog for him—"

"I was thinking more along the lines of you touching me back," he said. "Albeit reluctantly, of course."

She flushed as she realized he'd meant cooperation in the facade of seduction. For it was a facade, and she'd do well to remember that. Nevertheless, she put her arms around him, sliding them from his shoulders down his back to his waist. He let out short, compressed breath, as if that relatively innocent caress had somehow interfered with his normal breathing.

After a moment, he continued.

"I thought," he said against her throat, "that he'd just want me to steal the plans, and the supporting data and research."

She shifted, unable to stop herself; he might be able to compartmentalize and keep himself thinking coolly while he pretended to seduce her, but it was getting more difficult for her with every passing second. And she told herself that his quick intake of air as she moved beneath him meant nothing. It was all for show, for the man still too close by, and who would no doubt be back momentarily, watching them with an avidness that was beyond creepy.

"But?" she said, keeping it at the single, short word in an effort to hide the tangled emotions she was afraid might echo in her voice if she tried to say more.

He lowered his head to rest on her shoulder, his back to Arlen. "I had to stall him, try to find out if he'd already recruited his mole. But that gave him time to work his way into this self-righteous lather about how badly WhitSys—and you in particular—had treated him."

"I never—"

He hushed her with his mouth on hers again. It worked, too well, as heat rushed through her yet again. What the hell was wrong with her? She had no idea if any of this was even true. And even if it was, it didn't change the fact that this was faked. No matter which scenario was true—that he was a willing accomplice lying to try to get her to help them, or that he was indeed working for J.W.—this little seduction scene was all for show.

"I know," he said finally, after breaking off the kiss with every appearance of reluctance. "He's got a warped view of everything. You were the woman who spurned him. Also the woman who happens to have more access than anyone short of John Whitney himself. So when we met in the parking garage tonight, and he saw you…"

"Are you saying," she hissed against his throat, "that he just up and decided to grab me just because I was there?"

For a moment he didn't answer. Oddly, he'd tilted his head back, as if to offer his neck up to her mouth. *Lucky for you I'm not a vampire,* she thought.

The lame joke didn't banish the unwelcome wish that he would really want her mouth on him the way his had been all over her.

"Pretty much," he finally said. "He was fully pissed by then. I wasn't moving fast enough to suit him, and he was tired of waiting. And then you walked out of the elevator."

"Impulse."

"Yes. He's not a great thinker anyway, when you add in impulsive and season it with revenge, it's a dangerous mix." He gave that same half shrug. "Better me than him in that case."

It hit her then. "You…what? Volunteered?"

"It was the only way to make sure you didn't get hurt."

"But I thought you suspected I was already in on it."

"It was only a possibility. And not a strong one. So part of my job had to be making sure you didn't get hurt. John would kill me if anything happened to you."

She wasn't sure J.W. would ever kill anyone for any reason, but the words warmed her anyway. She wanted to ask more, know more, but at the moment processing his honorable actions was all she could manage. Arlen was so strung out over this that she had no doubts he would have done worse than backhand her if she'd made him angrier, which she seemed to be able to do without much effort.

As if her thoughts had produced him, she heard a sound that told her he was back in the doorway, watching again.

"Mmm," Kincaid said. And only then did she realize she'd reached up to brush her fingers over his cheek. He turned his head slightly and kissed her hand. She shivered. The awkward nerd was a distant memory, burned away by the sizzling presence of this lean, sexy, competent man.

This man she wanted to kiss again. And again.

He stared down at her, his eyes suddenly hot, his gaze even more intense, as if he'd somehow read the need building in her.

She brushed a thumb over his mouth. His tongue flicked out to taste it. She lifted her head, seeking. He lowered his. The air between them seemed to quiver, like some intimate mirage. She—

"That's enough!"

Arlen had moved, more quickly than she would have thought possible. Or she'd been more oblivious. She knew which one was more likely. Even Kincaid seemed caught off guard, jerking upright.

"Dammit," Kincaid muttered as one hand shot to the small of his back and came up empty. It wasn't clear if the curse was aimed at Arlen, or himself. And in the next instant Taylor realized it was probably both. Because Arlen wasn't just standing over them, his face contorted with rage.

He was standing over them with Kincaid's gun.

# Chapter 11

Taylor eyed Arlen apprehensively. She was still rubbing at her arm where he'd grabbed her and yanked her off the couch and back into the big office. Apparently watching Kincaid "work" on her had been well and good—until she started to respond. The simple gestures of sliding her hands down Kincaid's back, touching his cheek, then his mouth, of her own volition had lit the fuse of the man she'd once spurned.

Kincaid didn't seem to be treading warily himself.

"Give me my gun," he said, and it was nothing short of an order.

"You're not running this show, Kincaid," Arlen said. "Time you remembered that."

"I've never forgotten this is completely your idea and your operation," Kincaid said, flicking a glance at Taylor, telling her silently that those words were for her as much as Arlen. "But nobody else handles that weapon. It's precisely balanced and sighted for me. Anybody else would likely miss what they were aiming at."

Taylor didn't see how anybody could miss anything at a range of six feet. The thought didn't help any.

"You'll get it back. When she does what she's told."

"Take it easy, Arlen," Kincaid said. "She's going to cooperate."

*Like hell,* Taylor thought.

"Sit down," Arlen told her, gesturing toward the executive chair he'd been sitting in.

She did so, reluctantly, but embarrassingly aware her knees were a little wobbly at the moment. She found herself facing the screen of the laptop she'd noticed before. It was on, a screen saver shooting oddly twisted and bizarrely colored shapes that sort of resembled spiders doing gymnastics at her. It was a larger model, with a wider screen, making the images even more unsettling.

Arlen leaned over her and hit a key. The screen saver vanished. He used the touch pad and clicked on an icon. A familiar log-on screen appeared.

"Sign in," he ordered.

Pointing out that he shouldn't have the WhitSys internal software seemed a silly idea under the circumstances. Besides, this was a turn of events she didn't mind at all. But she decided it would be better if she didn't let that show.

"Why?" she asked instead.

"You're not that stupid. Sign on. It's going to take time to download Watchdog."

"It won't work."

"Just do it." He nudged her with the barrel of the gun.

She flicked a glance at Kincaid. He gave her a barely perceptible nod. She typed in her system name and a password. For a moment she held her breath. When the anticipated response came, she breathed again.

Arlen leaned in, staring at the chaos on the screen, window after window of random numbers and letters popping up. "What the hell is that?"

Taylor looked up at him, letting a bit of her satisfaction show in her face and echo in her voice. "You're a fool, Arlen. Did you really think we wouldn't install Watchdog on our own network? I told you this wouldn't work."

Kincaid leaned over her chair to take a look.

"What did you do?" Arlen demanded.

"It's all a matter of the right—or wrong—password."

She didn't hide the smugness she was feeling that Watchdog had worked perfectly. Kincaid moved closer. She glanced up at him, saw the tiny smile that lifted one corner of his mouth. While Arlen gaped at the laptop, he winked at her.

"Stop it!" Arlen shouted, gesturing wildly at the screen.

"Can't. This computer is locked out. Permanently. And even if you could get it to download, the program would be completely corrupted."

He glared at her. "That's not how Watchdog works."

"It is now," she said. "Mark programmed it to learn. Any new attempt at a breach and it automatically builds a new defense. No waiting around for updates, for other people to come up with threat solutions. Watchdog is more than you could ever in your pitiful life begin to imagine."

She was feeling more confident by the moment, inspired by her success at foiling any chance Arlen had of getting Watchdog, at least for now. And by the solid presence of Kincaid, who had once more managed to position himself in between her and the obviously furious Arlen.

"You don't know anything about how Watchdog works," she said, unable to resist the chance to needle him even further now that she knew Watchdog was safe from him. "What little you had to do with it, what tiny contribution you made turned out to be useless and was removed. Just like you."

Arlen moved then, another string of foul names spewing from him as he straightened up and turned to point the gun at her again, this time with deadly intent gleaming in crazed eyes. He moved fast, but Kincaid was faster. In the instant that Arlen moved, so did he, lashing out quickly, powerfully, with his forearm, driving Arlen's hand upward just as he pulled the trigger.

The shot echoed off the walls, louder than Taylor had ever imagined a shot could be. She barely stifled a scream in reaction to the sheer volume of it. Or in reaction to the reality that if not for Kincaid, Arlen would have actually shot her. Any lingering doubts she had about what side he was on vanished.

The two men grappled, Kincaid trying to wrest the weapon away from Arlen, who was struggling desperately to keep it. Taylor wasn't sure he realized yet he'd been betrayed, and in the next moment she knew he hadn't.

"What the hell are you doing, Kincaid?"

"Putting an end to this."

He sent an elbow upward, ramming it into Arlen's

throat. The man gagged, stumbled back, still hanging on to the weapon. Taylor jumped back as he sprawled across the desk.

Arlen brought the gun up, this time aiming it at Kincaid, but still looking puzzled; slow as ever, he hadn't completely comprehended his so-called partner was anything but.

Kincaid eyed Arlen. Taylor hoped he wasn't fool enough to charge a loaded weapon in a nervous and untrained hand. It suddenly occurred to her that while Arlen was focused on Kincaid, he wasn't looking at her. In fact, she was behind him.

She grabbed up the laptop, shutting it in the same motion. Arlen glanced toward her at the movement, but the gun was still trained on Kincaid.

She slammed the heavy laptop into his face.

The impact was oddly satisfying. So was the sight of Arlen sliding to the floor with a groan. Even more satisfying was the startled look Kincaid gave her, followed by a grin that nearly took her breath away.

"Nice work, elf," he said.

And as he bent to retrieve the pistol Arlen had dropped, Taylor thought that maybe she didn't really hate that nickname as much as she thought she did.

## Chapter 12

"You're sure you're all right?"

Taylor looked at her boss and nodded. "I'm fine."

"You're not angry with me?"

He sounded so anxious, Taylor couldn't help but smile. "No."

"I never, ever suspected you. And I hated lying to you. But he—"

"I know." She hesitated over what to call him. Then settled on formality. "Mr. Kincaid told me he was the one who wouldn't let you tell me what was going on."

"He was pretty adamant. I kept telling him there was no way, but…" At least this explained the sense she'd gotten that J.W. felt guilty; he had. About lying to her, if nothing else.

"I imagine in his line of work he has to be suspicious of everyone."

J.W. nodded, appearing relieved that she understood.

She wasn't sure she did, not really. There had been so much chaos afterward that she and Kincaid had barely had a chance to speak. Not that he had shown any inclination to speak. To her, anyway. He dealt with the mess, the police and their seemingly endless questions, the damage to the building, and notifying the owner of said building who had made the mistake of believing Arlen Sanders was actually a potential tenant. He did it all efficiently and professionally.

The police, she noticed, handled her with tact and gentleness. She was the real victim in all this, they said. They even kindly assured her that the shaking she couldn't seem to stop was a normal, typical reaction. Adrenaline crash, they called it. She'd done amazingly well, they said. Heroically, they said.

"Kincaid told us," the detective she spent nearly an hour with had said. As if that were enough.

"You…know him?" she'd asked.

"Of him," the woman had said. "He's got a reputation for honesty. And for getting things done."

*Unless he has to lie to you to get those things done,* she thought, but without any real anger.

That had been about all she'd been able to glean from the cops more bent on getting the facts sorted out. And to be fair, making sure she was all right.

She hadn't seen Kincaid at all. He'd been closeted with the other detective assigned to the case, or else they'd been keeping them separate to make sure their stories jibed, she wasn't sure which.

*Or maybe Kincaid just doesn't want to see you, so he's hiding out, avoiding any emotional fallout.*

In her weariness, the glum assessment had seemed the most likely. In any case, she clearly wouldn't get any answers from the man himself. So she turned now to her boss to answer her myriad questions.

"What *is* his line of work, exactly?"

J.W. shrugged, as if he were at a loss to explain. "He just…helps people out now and then."

"He said he wasn't exactly a private investigator."

"No. He's not. It's not that…formal, or official. He's just really good at solving puzzles, at figuring things out, and occasionally he does it for people in need."

"Occasionally?"

J.W. nodded. "He doesn't have to work unless he wants to. He made a lot of money, backing a friend who had an idea for a new kind of video-conferencing system. You know it as VirtualBoardroom."

Her brow furrowed. "Max Planter?" she asked.

"Yes," J.W. said. "They went to school together. Kincaid loaned him part of the money he used to get started."

She could only imagine how that had paid off; the system had become almost ubiquitous.

"That's who referred me to him," J.W. said. "That's the only way he works, referrals from others he's helped."

"But why?"

"He says he does it," J.W. said solemnly, "because years ago, when he was little more than a kid, he did some foolish things and got in some serious trouble. But somebody helped him when he needed it, and he straightened his life out. He's just passing it along."

*You should be ashamed of yourself.*

*Time was, I have been. But no more.*

The exchange that had occurred what seemed like eons ago echoed in her mind. She wondered who had helped him.

And she found she wasn't in the least surprised that he had, in the end, saved himself. It fit with the quiet strength she'd seen in him.

Later, as she sat in her office—door closed to stem the flow of stunned and curious people wanting to talk to her about what had happened—she allowed herself to think about it. There hadn't really been time before. J.W. had arrived at the police station shortly after 2:00 a.m., and had taken charge of her, seeing that she got out of there to get some rest. She'd been so exhausted by the time she'd gotten home that she'd fallen into bed and slept for nearly ten hours.

J.W. had told her not to come in for the rest of the week, but her curiosity had been too strong and she'd come in this afternoon anyway.

"Not that you know much more than you did before," she muttered to herself.

She turned to her computer and called up a search engine, barely noticing the day's gorgeous photograph and the attendant links to the tidbits of knowledge she usually enjoyed reading.

She entered his name.

The first thing she noticed was that, halfway around the world in the U.K., Angus Kincaid wasn't a rare name. But a quick scan of the offered links showed nothing particularly helpful, nothing she could even pin down as being related to *her* Angus Kincaid.

*Oh, please,* she thought. *He's not yours. He was playing a part because he had to. It's not his fault you lit up like a Christmas tree every time he touched you.*

She shut the browser and went back to work. Until the next time she weakened and went searching again.

For the next week, she spent far too much time

having to push the images out of her mind. She tried to work, but had problems finding her usual efficient focus. More than once she found herself digging more, working her way through those weblinks she'd found. Occasionally—but only occasionally—she spotted something. Never anything she could say with one hundred percent certainty was related to him, but possibilities. A post on a suicide hotline forum, about a man named Kincaid who had helped someone find out why their brother had done it. A blog entry about a man named Kincaid who had found a runaway child when the police hadn't been able to. There weren't many, and one indicated his desire to remain anonymous, which might explain the dearth of references.

And when she finally turned away from the seemingly fruitless task, she was always startled to realize how long she'd been digging. She had to snap out of this. Had to put him out of her mind and get back to work. Even her boss's prodigious patience could run out if she kept on like this.

J.W. was pushing her to see a counselor after her terrifying experience, but she kept putting him off. The last thing she wanted to do was face some stranger and maybe end up letting slip that she'd done the stupidest possible thing, and genuinely fallen for her white knight. One who had walked away without a backward glance, once the crisis was over.

Maybe she just needed to see him, talk to him. Maybe now, when she wasn't scared or in danger, she'd see that that was all it had been. Because of the situation, he'd become this heroic being in her mind, maybe she just needed to see him in reality, in everyday circumstances. Maybe without the fear-spiked adrenaline flooding her system she'd see him more clearly, realize her reaction to him had been disproportionate, and due to the circumstances.

Maybe.

Would he even talk to her? He hadn't even said goodbye, hadn't called to see how she was doing, hadn't even asked about her through J.W., because she knew her boss would have said something, he was so worried about her.

All right, so maybe she should call him. Ask him to meet with her, promise him it would be short, that she just needed…what? Closure? She hated the psychobabble word, but it was the only thing that came to mind.

J.W. would give her his number, she was sure he would. Maybe just talking to him on the phone would do it, she thought, brightening. He'll just be brisk and impersonal, kind but uninvolved, and she'd finally be able to put this all behind her and get back to her life.

That was it. She'd talk to him, and just his demeanor, which would be professional and nothing more, would help her yank herself back to reality. She would—

"Ms. Burke."

The voice came from her right and behind. She spun around in her chair, startled. And in the doorway to her boss's office stood the man who had been tormenting her thoughts for days on end.

# Chapter 13

Taylor wondered inanely if anybody in the office had even recognized him. Because this was the real Angus Kincaid, the one only she and, she guessed, J.W. had seen.

Dressed in a gray pair of khaki-style pants and a matching ribbed sweater, any resemblance to the disguise he'd adopted here was long gone, as was the awkward demeanor. This man exuded a quiet, steady sort of confidence, a quick intelligence and a barely leashed energy that made her wonder how she hadn't seen it before, no matter how well concealed.

He shut the door behind him and walked slowly into her office, a cup from J.W.'s coffee set up in his hand. She marveled anew at how he moved differently, the smooth, controlled motion diametrically opposed to the jerky, fumbling movements of the office drone.

As he crossed her office she stood up, not sure why, but wanting to be on her feet.

*To run?* she chided herself, acknowledging the irony of the urge to flee after spending a week wishing she could see him.

Her usually quick and agile mind floundered, and when he came to a halt a bare three feet away and just looked at her, she blurted out the first stupid thing she could find words for.

"Plain coffee?"

He got there instantly. "All I drink, contrary to… appearances."

So it had been affectation, the fancy drinks.

"Do your friends really just call you Kincaid?" She nearly groaned inwardly. *Nice non sequitur, Burke. So what's the third stupid thing you're going to say?*

He didn't give her the look she deserved. "Mostly," he said. "Only the closest call me Kin."

"Who calls you Angus?"

"No one who wants to call again," he said dryly.

The wry humor unknotted the tension inside her a bit.

"I— It's good to see you," she said, wondering if she was doomed to complete inanity around this man.

"You look good," he said, and it took everything she had to make herself believe the unspoken addendum was "after what you've been through," rather than "I missed you."

"So do you," she said, keeping her tone neutral with a tremendous effort, and striving for some kind of normal conversation. "If I didn't know, I doubt I'd recognize you, now."

"Give people something predictable to focus on, and they often miss the rest."

"I always thought there was more to you than what I saw, but everything I heard and found out supported your…cover. I decided I must be wrong."

"John told me you seemed…disappointed when he gave you the story we'd concocted." A new undertone had come into his voice, as if he were pleased that, even slightly, she'd seen more than anyone else.

"I was. But you played it so perfectly…"

"I've gotten pretty good at it, over the years."

"I noticed." She gave herself a mental shake. "I should thank you for what you did. For helping us."

"John already has."

"And paid you?" she asked. "Do I need to cut a check?" She wondered how much you paid a man for doing what he'd done.

"He already made a nice donation to a private charity I selected. That's what I charge people."

She blinked. "What?"

"I don't need the money."

"So J.W. said. But you do this for nothing?"

"Not for nothing. Some things offend my sense of order, and need to be set right. And I only take cases that move me to that."

*Damn.*

She had hoped seeing him again would help her get over this silly infatuation. Instead, he'd shown up and made himself even more appealing. He truly was some sort of white knight, riding to the rescue.

*And then riding off into the sunset,* she reminded herself.

"John tells me you're efficient, practical and that you don't beat around the bush," he said.

She stared at him. Not about the assessment, which

she supposed was accurate, but at the fact that he'd been discussing her at all.

"True?" he asked.

His gaze was fixed on her steadily, and she remembered for a moment that sense of shock when she'd seen his eyes for the first time, without the heavy glasses. They really were an incredible blue, she thought.

"I suppose," she said, suddenly realizing he was waiting for an answer.

"Then I'll be direct."

He paused, and she saw him suck in a breath. He looked almost...nervous, she thought, although her common sense—something that had seemed strangely absent in the past few days—told her that was unlikely.

"I've spent the last week working harder than I have in a long time," he finally said. "And I haven't gotten anywhere. I keep backsliding, and no matter how much I try, I can't seem to break free."

"Free of what?"

He took another deep breath. Kept his gaze fastened on her, saying bluntly, "You."

Taylor nearly gasped aloud.

"I've told myself it was just situational. Adrenaline and all that. Then I told myself that I just admired you for how you defended John, how you stood up to Sanders. All of which is true."

Taylor opened her mouth to speak, then shut it again when she realized she had no idea what to say.

"Then," he said, his voice changing, taking on that husky note she'd heard when he'd been setting her blood boiling, "I tried to convince myself that it wasn't what it had felt like, that kissing you, touching you hadn't really been the most incredibly, impossibly, searingly hot thing that I'd ever done."

The memories nearly swamped her, and this time she did gasp aloud, she couldn't help herself. But any coherent words seemed beyond her, and she could only gape at him.

"And when I asked you to play along in that little scene, I never expected it to practically take the top of my head off when you did. You just touched me and I…"

For the first time since he'd come in, he looked away. Lowered his gaze from her face, as if he didn't want to see it when he said his next words. That in itself amazed her anew; she doubted he went out of his way to avoid much of anything.

"Then I told myself if you…had any interest, you'd let me know."

Taylor was stunned at what she was hearing. That he'd spent the past week in the same confusion that she had. A million words rose to her lips, but she still couldn't seem to get any of them out.

"Then I told myself I'd get over it, if I just stayed away."

Taylor finally found her voice. "It didn't work for me," she said softly.

His gaze shot back to her face. "Taylor?"

She put everything she thought into the look she gave him, everything she felt into the smile. And when she spoke, she let it all pour into her voice.

"Elf will do," she said. "I've decided that from the right person, I rather like it."

He crossed the distance between them in a stride that was almost a leap. He grabbed her shoulders, held them with that strength she remembered, that had been so startling then.

"You mean it?"

"In addition all those other sterling qualities John mentioned," she said with a self-deprecating smile, "I also have a tendency to say what I mean and mean what I say."

"Hallelujah," he said, pulling her into the embrace she'd wanted since the moment he'd appeared.

She resisted the urge to say, "Amen."

And then, looking down at her intently, his voice quiet, he asked, "You felt it, too? You weren't just… playing along?"

She smiled rather wryly. "I've spent the past week trying to convince myself that's what you'd been doing."

"I wasn't," he said. "I never expected…what happened." His mouth quirked. "How could I, when I've never felt anything like it before?"

She reached up then, brushed his cheek as she had that day. And as he had that day, he turned his head and kissed her fingers. And as it had that day, it sent a shiver through her that was deliciously hot and cold at the same time.

"I never knew anything like that was even possible," she said. "And no matter how often I told myself I was only reacting so strongly because you were saving me, it didn't matter."

He drew back, grinned at her; it took her breath away. "Saving you? As I recall, you're the one who gave Sanders a concussion with that laptop."

"I should have hit his foul mouth, not his nose."

He laughed. She loved the sound of it.

He loosened his arms, but didn't let go. "I ruined your Valentine's Day," he said.

She drew back slightly. "That reminds me. That card. How did you know how I feel about that?"

"John told me."

The simplest of explanations were often true, she thought. She smiled. "It was hardly ruined, considering."

One day, she thought, maybe she'd tell him how often she'd read and reread that card he'd given her.

"Let me make up for it."

"All right," she said simply.

She didn't know if he'd expected to have to coax her or persuade her, but his smile was instant and warm. And then, with slow, gentle care, he kissed her.

She'd almost been dreading the moment, afraid that what had flashed unexpectedly to life between them in their dangerous ordeal had been born only of those moments. The first touch of his mouth on hers shattered her fears into dust; the fire leaped to life as if it had never been banked.

When he finally broke away, she felt so wobbly she had to lean against him.

"Proof?" he whispered.

"Conclusive, Kincaid," she agreed.

He chuckled. "You'd better start calling me Kin now. Save time."

*Only the closest call me Kin.*

"What if I want to call you Angus?" she teased.

He winced, then sighed. "Then I'll answer. An exception I wouldn't make for anyone else."

The admission told her everything she wanted to know.

And Taylor Burke realized that perhaps, just perhaps, she didn't loathe Valentine's Day after all.

* * * * *

# THE FEBRUARY 14TH SECRET

## Cindy Dees

This book is dedicated to everyone who thinks love will never happen to them. Love yourself, love life, and remember love may be waiting just around the corner for you. From my heart to yours, Happy Valentine's Day.

# Chapter 1

The Valentine's Day card—from a dead man—slipped out of Layla's numb fingers and fluttered to the floor. *No. It couldn't be.* Peter had been gone for months. She'd been to his *open-casket* funeral in their hometown, Sturgeon's Corners, Oregon. In fact, his funeral was just about the only thing on earth that could drag her back to that god-forsaken place.

Peter. Was. Dead.

And yet…

She bent over and picked up the card, touching it reluctantly, as if it might bite her at any moment. She opened it and read the message again in the familiar and distinctive spiky handwriting.

*Happy V-Day, Lulu,*
*You up for our annual feeling-sorry-for-us dinner?*
*Let's do it up big—The Pleasant Peasant, seven*

*o'clock, on Valentine's Day weekend—Friday night.*
*Lots of annoyingly content couples to hex. We've*
*got a lot to talk about.*
*Love, P.*

It had to be him. No one in the world but Peter called her Lulu. And who else would know about their annual Valentine's tradition of going to the most romantic restaurant they could find and jokingly cursing all the blissfully romantic couples around them to have miserable love lives? A chill crawled up her spine. How could a dead man invite her to dinner?

Layla looked around the funky San Francisco restaurant nervously. Despite its carefully eclectic decor and elegantly vegetarian menu, The Pleasant Peasant was still a hippie joint at heart. The waiters wore tie-dye T-shirts and long hair pulled back into ponytails. Bongs sat on high shelves around the room, and photographs of peace protests, love-ins and Woodstock lined the walls. This had always been Peter's favorite restaurant in the Bay area. She hadn't been back here since he'd gone missing last year at right about this time, in fact, in some tiny central Asian country. Something-*i-stan*.

Who was she about to face now? She'd considered every possibility, from Peter having elaborately faked his death, to him returning from the dead as a vampire. Perhaps in his supersecret research for the U.S. government, he had learned how to temporarily suspend life.

"May I refill your glass?" a waiter asked, startling her badly.

"Uh, sure," she mumbled.

The waiter poured her a bloodred pomegranate cock-tail. She hoped the gruesome-looking drink wasn't prophetic of things to come. Her watch said it was almost seven o'clock. She had a weird premonition something life-changing was about to happen. Her heart started to pound and her body felt hot and feverish.

Trying not to stare at the entrance, she nonetheless gaped when the unlikeliest possible person stepped inside. People here would call him "The Man." And they wouldn't mean it as a compliment. The patron looked like a soldier who'd tried completely unsuccessfully to disguise himself as a civilian. His hair was dark and short, his spine rigid, his bearing distinctly military. Even his tie looked uptight, all stiff and perfectly knotted. He must have lost a bet to have wound up in this place, which catered to the Haight-Ashbury district's most liberal elements.

The misfit was tall and muscular beneath that suit. Not her type, but seriously built in spite of the whole *Dragnet* cop impersonation. With a little more hair and a whole lot less spit and polish, she might even consider photographing him. She looked away as the stranger's piercing gaze roamed across the restaurant.

A moment later, a voice spoke quietly beside her. "Layla?"

Her heart in her throat, she looked up and froze. The tall, dark, military man loomed over her. Who *was* this guy? And how did he know her name?

"I'm Colt McQuade. Peter sent me."

Peter? Was he *alive?* What had the military done with him? She leaped to her feet, her heart racing in staccato panic. "How?" she demanded. "Who are you? Where's Peter? What has happened to him?" Other patrons stared as she asked rapid-fire tense questions at the big man.

"Why don't we sit down?" McQuade suggested carefully, his voice obviously pitched to soothe the crazy woman. "I'll explain over dinner."

She settled into her chair warily as the man took the seat opposite her at the tiny table. He was too rugged for a movie star but had a hint of old Hollywood glamour to him. He'd look good on black-and-white film. Use of shadows would be important in the photograph composition to catch the hard angles of his face and cold, intelligent calculation in his clear brown eyes.

She drained her glass and set it down a tad too hard. "Where's Peter?" she demanded more quietly. "Is he all right? Did he send me that card?"

"I suppose he did send it in a manner of speaking," McQuade answered cryptically.

"What does that mean? Where is he?"

"Do you ever ask just one question at a time?" her companion asked dryly.

She scowled, and he responded, "Peter said you were impatient. If you'll just hold your horses, ma'am, I'll try to answer all your questions. But I think it would be best if I start at the beginning."

"What beginning?" This man was speaking as if Peter was definitely alive! A glimmer of excitement bubbled up in her chest.

A smile danced at the corner of his mouth for a moment as if he found her impatience amusing. Peter used to half smile at her just like that, too. Something…odd…skated through her. It felt like walking over someone's grave.

"As I said, my name's Colt McQuade. I'm from Oklahoma originally. I joined the army thirteen years ago. Most recently, I worked with a Special Forces unit. We got deployed to Kyrgyzstan last year. On Valentine's Day."

*That was it. Kyrgyzstan. The place where Peter had died.* McQuade's tea arrived and he was silent while the waiter poured it for him. She wouldn't have pegged G.I.

Joe for a tea drinker. Maybe he'd picked up the habit in Central Asia. McQuade fiddled with his teabag until it looked for all the world like he was stalling.

She prompted, "Kyrgyzstan?"

A dark shadow passed through his eyes. "Right. Kyrgyzstan. I can't go into the details of the mission, but suffice it to say things didn't go well. I got captured."

"By whom?" she asked, startled.

"Local crime boss. Name's not important. He tossed me into a hole and left me to rot. It was some sort of underground cellar. At any rate, there was this guy already down there before me."

Layla leaned forward. "Peter?"

"Yeah. Peter Morrison."

The waiter interrupted again, this time to hand them menus. It took Colt about five seconds perusing the veggie menu to grimace. Must be a hardcore carnivore. They ordered, and then Layla prodded McQuade to continue. "You were in a cellar. With Peter."

"Right. He was in rough shape."

"Translation?" she asked grimly.

"Physically, he was pretty beat-up. Mentally, he was losing his grip on reality. He and I talked a lot. I don't know if it helped him or not. In the end, they pushed him too far." McQuade added reluctantly, "Translation—he couldn't take what they dished out."

McQuade said no more. He merely stared blankly into his teacup. He might as well be a thousand miles away. "Then what?" she asked quietly.

He looked up sharply, startled. "What?"

"What happened to Pete?"

"Oh. Right."

Speaking of lost marbles, she was beginning to have

her doubts about this guy having all of his. Maybe coming to this dinner had been a bad idea. "Well?" she asked.

A shrug. "He died from his injuries."

Layla's hopes fell off a cliff and dashed to pieces on the rocky shores of reality. Peter was really dead, then? "But the card... That was his handwriting. I'm sure of it!"

"You're right. He told me he'd written you a Valentine's card but didn't get to send it before he left for Kyrgyzstan. He expected to mail it when he got home. I took the liberty of going over to his place and finding it. I mailed it to you."

"You shouldn't have sent it to me," she said low and furious. "You got my hopes up for nothing. It was a cruel joke."

McQuade blinked a few times and then the skin around his eyes tightened grimly. "Believe me, ma'am. This is no joke. I *had* to be sure you'd come tonight and talk to me."

"Why? What could be so important that you had to drag me through the emotional wringer like this?"

McQuade leaned forward and, matching her intensity, replied, "If it makes you feel better, it was Peter who sent me to you. And it's a matter of national security for you and me to figure out why."

She stared. "What on God's green earth are you talking about?"

"If you'll let me continue, that's what I'm trying to explain."

She pursed her lips. "Then, by all means, continue."

It was his turn to scowl. "Peter and I spent a lot of time together. When our captors weren't busy interrogating or torturing one of us, of course. Toward the end things got really bad, and that was when Peter did something to me."

She stared at the powerful man before her and recalled her scrawny, uncoordinated friend. Surely Peter couldn't have dented this guy, let alone hurt him.

McQuade was speaking again. "I don't know what he did. Some sort of hypnosis. But whatever he did, I'm hauling around a piece of him inside me, now."

Layla stared. And then she laughed in disbelief. "Are you talking about a Vulcan mind-meld?"

It was McQuade's turn to stare. And then he spoke very slowly, as if to a child. "You do know Vulcans aren't real, right?"

"Yeah, I got that memo," she retorted. "More's the pity. Vulcans are emotionally stable, predictable, so much easier to deal with than human men."

McQuade just shook his head.

Exasperated at his inability to maintain a thread of conversation, she said, "So Peter did his hoojey-moojey on you. Then what?"

"The torture got worse. He couldn't take it anymore. His body gave way under the pressure. He lost his will to live."

Pain speared through her. It was one thing to suspect that Peter's death had been awful. It was another to learn for certain that she'd been correct. At least Peter hadn't been alone at the end. He'd had this grouchy soldier with him. It was better than nothing, she supposed. Silence fell between them. She picked at the excellent dinner, but her heart wasn't in the meal. Poor Peter. His life might have been troubled, but he didn't deserve such a tragic end.

Her dinner companion wasn't faring much better with his meal, either. Eventually, she pushed back her plate and asked soberly, "What possessed you to send me that Valentine's Day card? How did you know I'd show up?"

McQuade shrugged. "We had a lot of time on our hands. Peter told me pretty much everything about his life. And you were a very large part of it. He said you're the curious sort. Can't resist a good mystery."

Layla blinked, alarmed. How much did this man know about her? She'd confided everything in Peter. He'd known about or participated in pretty much all of her most private and personal secrets. Surely Peter hadn't shared all of those with this complete stranger. He'd better not have or she'd kill him—oh, wait. Peter was already dead. Her indignation broke on a wave of grief.

A large, hard hand closed over hers on the table. Her fingers suddenly felt small and girly by comparison. McQuade murmured, "I'm sorry for your loss. Peter had a good heart. He loved you more than anyone else in the whole world."

She didn't need this soldier boy to tell her that! She jerked her hand away from the disturbing contact. She would get up and leave right now except this man knew everything about Peter's final days. A compulsion to know all the details of her friend's end held her reluctantly in her seat.

He said wryly, "Would it make you feel better to curse a few of the blissfully happy couples around us to have terrible relationship troubles this coming year?"

She smiled, but it didn't dry the tears in her heart. "No. That's okay. I think my Valentine's Day is going to suck enough this year to make up for all the happy couples here."

McQuade said quietly, "I know the feeling. I've been dreaming about Peter. And it's getting worse. It's as if he's trying to tell me something."

"Peter's trying to tell you something?" She echoed. "Dead Peter? He's *talking* to you from beyond the grave? Like a ghost?" She was stunned that this soldier believed something like that. Even she had a hard time believing it, and she was the new-age hippie of the two of them.

McQuade huffed. "I don't know what's going on. That's why I need your help."

"Why me?" she retorted. "I'm no expert in possession or communication with the dead."

"But you are an expert on Peter Morrison, and I need you to help me unlock whatever Peter hid inside my head."

"And you think it's a matter of national security?" she asked skeptically. "Why?"

"That's classified. Need to know only."

Whatever the heck that meant. Apparently the military jargon translated into a big, fat, not-gonna-tell-ya.

"I really don't see how I can be of any assistance to you, Mr. McQuade—"

"Please," he interrupted. "I'm desperate."

Him? Desperate? He looked totally calm, cool and collected. "Look. This has been a fascinating meal and thank you for filling in the details of Peter's last days. But I really don't think I can help you. Have a nice life, Mr. McQuade."

Under normal circumstances she'd have insisted on paying her half of the bill for dinner, but these were hardly normal circumstances. She got up from the table and headed for the exit, shamelessly sticking him with the tab. But hey. He'd tricked her into coming here in the first place. He could pay for dinner.

She hurried out of the restaurant. She wanted to be well away from here before McQuade came out. She headed for the nearest trolley stop, which was several blocks from the restaurant. It was a dark, misty evening and she huddled deeper into her coat as tendrils of fog reached out with cold fingers to caress her cheeks.

A shadow moved just ahead of her and she'd started, alarmed, before she realized it was just a man. He turned to walk in the same direction she was going. No big deal.

She thought she heard a new noise and glanced over her shoulder. In the dark and fog she couldn't make out anything more than a pair of distant shapes. Just two more people hurrying to their warm, dry homes on a cold, miserable evening.

But then out of nowhere a figure barreled at her out of an alley to her left. In the blink of an eye, the other three pedestrians had closed in on her and the attacker, forming a terrifying phalanx around her. Panic clenched her throat so tightly no sound came out when she tried to scream.

Abruptly, a male voice echoed weirdly out of the fog from behind them all. "Get away from her! It's me you want!"

Her assailants released her abruptly and spun toward Colt McQuade sweeping down upon them like an avenging angel out of the night…or, maybe more accurately, like a fullback charging a wall of defensive linemen. The effect of the collision between him and the four men was about the same as at a professional football game. With a tremendous crash, bodies went flying and grunts accompanied men being flung every which way.

A powerful hand gripped her upper arm. "Let's go, Layla," McQuade bit out.

"Who—"

"Later."

McQuade ducked into the alley her first attacker had come from and sprinted like the hounds of hell were after them, dragging her along beside him. Who were those men? And why had they jumped her? They hadn't reached for her purse or mauled her in any way. What had they wanted?

Footsteps pounded behind them.

They reached the end of the alley and McQuade yanked her left, racing down the next block so fast she barely stayed on her feet. Another turn, a suicidal dash across the street through oncoming traffic, one more block, and then McQuade was tearing open a car door and shoving her inside. He raced around to the driver's side, leaped in and peeled away from the curb.

She tried to catch her breath while McQuade drove like a stunt man, weaving through traffic at high speed and scaring her nearly as much as those four men had. Finally he slowed, and just like that, they blended into the Oakland-bound traffic, just another blue Prius on a Friday night.

"What. Was that. About?" she panted.

He glanced over at her grimly. "Believe me now when I say I need your help?"

"The way you took out those guys, it didn't look you needed much help to me," she replied sourly. "Who are they?"

"I don't know. But I think Peter knows."

"Peter's dead," she snapped.

"Not all of him. A piece of him is still in here." McQuade tapped his head. "And that piece might know."

"Then why not ask him?"

"Like a séance?" He made a scoffing noise.

"So you're going to channel him directly then?"

"I highly doubt that. I was thinking more in terms of

you figuring out what the trigger is to release the memory or whatever it is Peter stuck in my mind."

She shook her head. "This is too weird for me."

McQuade laughed, but the sound was devoid of any humor. "Hell, you ought to try living with a time bomb ticking inside your head. Sometimes I think I'm going crazy."

*Sometimes?* She was pretty darned sure the guy was fully there. "Can't the government help you? They've got doctors—specialists—who could handle something like this."

He sighed. "TV shows with far-out science in secret government labs aren't real."

"I *know* that," she groused. "But surely they've got shrinks who can deal with hypnotic suggestion or whatever this is."

"I've already talked to those guys. They think it's more akin to a post-traumatic stress reaction and will pass with time."

She exhaled hard in relief. "Well, there you have it. Go sit on a beach for a few months until your fantasies of Peter in your noggin go away."

"Been there, done that. Didn't work."

"Try harder," she suggested.

He threw her a withering look. "Trust me. You're my last resort."

Colt glanced across the car at the woman beside him. Peter hadn't been wrong about one thing. Layla Freeman was a hell of a looker. Those big blue eyes of hers went right through a guy, and all that creamy skin and swirling honey hair begged a man to touch them. Of course, she was every bit as stubborn as Peter had said, too. And that was a problem.

He seriously did need her help, and he was desperate enough to force her to do it. But he sensed that the harder he pushed her, the harder she would push back.

"Where are we going?" she asked.

"At the moment, away from where our pursuers will look for us."

"Us?" she squawked. "Why are those guys looking for me all of a sudden?"

"Because they saw you with me," he replied grimly.

"Surely you're exaggerating. Maybe along with your post-traumatic stress you're experiencing a teensy bit of paranoia?"

It would be so much easier if that were true. But he'd been dodging this team of men for nearly a week now. It was their relentless pursuit that had finally driven him to seek Layla's help in solving the mystery of whatever the hell Peter had planted in his head. If Colt had doubted the importance of whatever it was before, the fact that those men tonight had been willing to assault an innocent woman over it spoke volumes about how important it was. *What the hell did you do to me, Pete?*

"Colt, I want no part of this. Take me home."

"I don't think that's a good idea," he replied on a sigh.

"And I don't think it's your call to make," she snapped.

He really didn't want to kidnap her, but it might come down to that if he couldn't talk her into helping him voluntarily. "Fine," he replied reluctantly.

He guided the car toward her apartment, and thankfully, she didn't freak out that he knew where she lived. Maybe she remembered that he'd mailed the Valentine's card to her and seen her address on it.

As they neared her place, he slowed down and turned

off his headlights. The Prius shifted fully to its electric power train and rolled forward in near-total silence.

He murmured, "Indulge me. I'd like to watch your place for a few minutes before you go in. Just a precaution, you understand." Although he full well expected it was no precaution at all. He'd spent long enough barely staying one step ahead of his pursuers to know they were very, very good. He had complete confidence they had already identified Layla and were at her place learning everything they could about her.

She harrumphed but didn't protest. Maybe she had more sense than he gave her credit for. He found a parking space across the street and pulled into it. Silence fell in the car.

"What are we looking for?" she murmured eventually.

"Any sign that someone's inside your place. A light. A shadow passing in front of a window."

Abrupt fear rolled off her. He sighed. "Look. I'm sorry I dragged you into this. I tried to stay away from you. Keep you out of it. Out of respect for Peter's feelings for you."

"What, exactly, did he tell you of his feelings for me?" she asked tartly.

He winced. He'd been hoping this particular subject wouldn't come up between them. "You have to understand. We were stressed and isolated and didn't have another human being to talk to for months."

"What did he tell you?" she asked again with a note of alarm in her voice now.

"Everything," he answered simply.

Her luminous eyes went wide with horror. And with good cause. He knew every intimate, embarrassing, silly, sweet thing Peter could recall of her entire life. And Pete and Layla had been best friends since first grade. Peter had known *all* the dirt on her. In fact, meeting Layla tonight had been damned strange. It was as if he'd known her for years, and yet it was the first time he'd ever laid eyes on her.

"It's a darn good thing that rat fink is already dead," Layla mumbled in a strangled voice.

"I swear I'll take it all to my grave if that makes you feel any better," he said sincerely.

"This is shaping up to be the worst Valentine's Day *ever*," she grumbled mostly to herself.

He opened his mouth to speak, but then a movement caught his eye.

"Did you see that?" she gasped.

"Yes." That had definitely been a silhouette passing in front of her living-room window. Inside her apartment. A light went on in what was probably her bedroom and she gasped again. "We've got to call the police! I'm being robbed."

"They're not robbing you. They're searching for clues to Peter's secret and learning everything they can about you so they can find you. If you called the police, these guys would mow through an unsuspecting cop like grass."

"What are we going to do?"

Thank God. She was using the term *we*. He started the car and eased out of the parking space. "First order of business is to get out of here. Then we go to ground, figure out how to retrieve Peter's secret and discover why professional killers are so hot and bothered to get their hands on it."

"Easy-peasy, cheddar cheesy," she muttered.

"Okey-dokey, artichokey," he replied automatically.

She looked over at him, wide-eyed. "Peter always used to say that."

"Like you said," Colt replied grimly, "Vulcan mind-meld."

# Chapter 2

They made it all the way to the parking lot of a hotel north of San Francisco before it dawned on Layla that she had nothing but the clothes on her back with her. "Ohmigosh!" she exclaimed. "What am I going to do for clothes or a toothbrush or…" she stopped, embarrassed.

"Clean underwear?" her companion supplied dryly.

"Well, yes," she mumbled.

"That's why I brought us to a decent hotel. There'll be toiletries in the room. As for clothes, I've got cash. I'll take you shopping tomorrow."

Under normal circumstances, she might relish spending this man's money out of general principles, but they'd already established that nothing about this night was normal. He murmured to her to keep quiet while he checked them in. She was stunned when he claimed they were married, gave a fake name to the desk clerk, and then proceeded to produce a driver's license bearing that same name. Who was this guy? Was *he* really Colt McQuade at all? Was he actually the bad guy?

It didn't help matters when he leaned close to the clerk, whispered mysteriously, and then slid a folded hundred-dollar bill across the counter to the guy. Deep misgivings about being alone with this stranger in a hotel room rolled over her. As he led her across the lobby toward an elevator, she gave in to her fears and balked. "I think this may not be a good idea, Mr. McQuade. I don't know you at all."

"I can't be any worse than Tony Mastraconi."

Layla scowled. She'd gone to high school with Tony, and the jerk had been convinced he was entitled to any girl he wanted. Peter had valiantly stood up once to Tony under the bleachers at a pep rally on her behalf. It was why her best friend had a bridge and two false front teeth. "Okay, fine. So you know stuff about my past that only Peter would know. That doesn't necessarily make you a good guy. You could be one of Peter's interrogators for all I know."

"Yeah, except those men who jumped you, jumped me, too."

"Could've been staged."

She glared at him and he stared back frustrated. They were at an impasse. Finally, he sighed. Reached behind his waist and underneath his jacket. "If I wear these, would that make you feel better?" He raised his hand and a pair of metal handcuffs dangled from his index finger.

*He had handcuffs under his coat?* "There are so many comments I could make in response to your having those I don't know where to start," she groused.

She snatched the cuffs, and he turned around, grinning without comment, holding his hands behind his back. She snapped them on his wrists. As they stepped into the elevator, he commented wryly, "Only in this town could a woman cuff a man in a hotel lobby and nobody say a blessed thing about it."

"Welcome to San Francisco," she muttered as she followed him onto the elevator.

They got to the room and she took the key card out of his hand. The lock clicked and she pushed the door open. Colt followed her inside. Without prompting, he moved over to the king-size bed and sat down on the edge of it. She moved to the window, facing him cautiously.

"Okay, Mr. McQuade. Start talking."

"Please, call me Colt." She shrugged, and he continued, "I've told you most of what I can. I need your help extracting whatever memories Peter planted in my head before those jokers who attacked you catch up with us."

"And I already told you, I have no idea how to help you."

He gazed directly into her eyes. "We'll figure it out together."

A strange little shiver rippled down her spine. *Together, huh?* Good thing he was entirely not her type. She went for artsy, eccentric men. Of course, those guys had an unfortunate tendency to drift into the bed of the next interesting female who happened across their path. Hence, her perpetual single state.

"Where did Peter hide his secrets when he was a kid?" Colt asked, interrupting her reverie.

She frowned. "On his computer, mostly. He had an electronic journal. But he used to brag that the encryption to get into it was better than the stuff the Pentagon uses."

Colt snorted. "Knowing him, I can believe that. However, I'm told the government has already read his journals. There's no sign of what we're looking for in there. What about objects or things he wanted to keep secret? Where did he hide those?"

"What kind of objects?"

"Drugs. Condoms. Porn magazines. Whatever teenaged boys want to keep their parents from confiscating."

She laughed. "That may be what you were hiding. Peter didn't do drugs or girls. To my knowledge, he never hid anything at home. He didn't have an exactly warm and trusting relationship with his parents."

"My impression was he didn't have a warm and trusting relationship with anyone except you," Colt replied gently.

A flare of loss seared her soul. God, she missed Peter. She whispered, "Was he in pain when he died?"

Agony glinted dagger sharp in Colt's eyes. He shook his head in mute denial, but his eyes said it all. Oh, Lord. It had been worse than she'd imagined. Tears rolled down her cheeks. Colt half rose as if to comfort her, but she shrank away from him. He subsided with a sigh, as if interpreting her movement to be one of fear.

It wasn't, though. She didn't dare let anyone put their arms around her or give her permission to be weak. Once the dam opened, she wasn't sure she'd be able to get it shut again against the flood of grief tenuously held at bay. Peter had been the other half of her. Her soul mate in every way but one.

She curled up on the far side of the big bed, lost in sad memories. To his credit, McQuade was silent, respecting her misery. The hour grew late, and sand replaced the tears in her eyes. She didn't mean to do it, but her eyelids drifted closed and she fell asleep, the stress of the bizarre evening finally catching up with her.

Colt watched Layla, studying her features, memorizing the sweet line of her cheek, the soft fall of gold-tipped lashes against her porcelain skin. She was even more lovely in sleep when suspicion and doubt weren't crowding her gaze. Hard to believe that Peter and she hadn't been lovers. If she'd been *his* best friend forever, he damn well would have—

He broke off the thought. Not what he was here for. Exhaustion dragged at him. He'd been on the run continuously for days. He'd been catching naps in snatches here and there, but it was about time for him to go down for a solid eight hours if he was going to maintain any kind of combat effectiveness.

Thing was, he was still handcuffed. He could wake up Layla and ask her to unlock him, but there was no guarantee she'd do it even if he asked. He kicked off his shoes and stretched out on his side of the big bed. She hugged the far side of it, her back turned to him. She smelled good. He inhaled the soft vanilla-cookie scent of her and rolled to his stomach to ease the strain on his shoulders. *God, it felt good to be horizontal on a real bed and smelling a beautiful woman*. That was his last thought before he passed out.

How long he slept before the nightmares claimed him, he had no idea. He just knew that he was in a stone-walled room with his captors once more.

*They'd learned early to tie his hands and feet lest he break the unwary nose or wreck the nearest knee. Waves of fury rolled through him as they ran through the usual warm-up routine—beating, burning and electrocution. Kid stuff as torture went. The door opened just out of range of his swollen, split eyes.*

*Khan stepped into view. He was the sickest bastard Colt had ever had the misfortune to run across. Now, this man understood torture. Fear rippled through Colt, making his entire body shake reflexively in anticipation. Khan was a true master at inflicting pain, and furthermore, enjoyed the hell out of it. As Khan reached for his filleting knives, Colt couldn't help the tearing panic that screamed at his body to fight or flee. He fought his bonds, struggling futilely against the suffering to come. Dante's inferno had nothing on hell according to Khan.*

*The knife laid into his skin, peeling a strip from the flesh beneath, and he screamed. A heavy weight landed on him, holding him down and he struggled more wildly against the ropes.*

*Weight on his chest. He fought harder. Rolled to his back.*

*Something smacked Colt sharply across the cheek, although it barely registered compared to the other torture his body was suffering. Not a chance he would wake up voluntarily. His only refuge from Khan was this stolen moment of unconsciousness. The horror of the insults to his body threatened to overwhelm him and darkness crept forward. He strained toward it.* Blessed oblivion.

*Another sharp slap snapped his head the other direction.*

"Dammit, Colt. Wake *up!*"

*Crap. He knew the drill. They would douse him in cold water and electrocute him next to wake him. His temporary respite from hell was over. If only his hands were free. He yanked desperately on his bonds.*

*Hands held his shoulders down, cupped his face, shaking urgently.* "Look at me!"

Reluctantly, he blinked his eyes open. *What the heck?* Not Khan. Not even a man. The biggest, bluest eyes he'd ever seen stared down at him, and the distinct swell of a perfectly shaped breast was about a foot away from his face. As dirty thoughts ripped through his head, he jerked his gaze up to those stunning, blue-on-blue eyes. Man, he could get lost in that sapphire ocean and gladly drown in it. Had he died? Gone to heaven?

Layla watched warily as Colt roused slowly from his tactical nuclear nightmare. How in the heck he'd come to be in bed beside her she had no idea, but at least he was still safely handcuffed. It was probably the only thing keeping him from killing her at the moment. The guy was clearly having some sort of hallucination or flashback.

She all but sobbed in relief when his eyes finally opened. "Layla?" he whispered tentatively, almost like he didn't believe she was real.

"Thank God. You were having a bad dream."

"What are you doing on top of me?"

"Trying to keep you from hurting yourself. What were you dreaming about?"

His gaze went hard but remained haunted. It tore at her heart to see the pain his dark, opaque gaze.

"Please, Layla. You have to help me. I can't do this alone."

What did he mean? That he couldn't open up the secrets in his mind without her? Or something more sinister? Like he was losing his grip on reality? Or that he wasn't strong enough to fight off their attackers alone? Scary thought. She couldn't imagine anyone stronger than this warrior of a man.

"What do those men want from you?" she asked.

"They want the information Peter put in my mind. Whatever it is, it's obviously important or Pete wouldn't have gone to so much trouble to hide it in my mind."

"Did he tell you anything at all about what he put there?" she prompted when he didn't continue.

"He said he put it in a jar." Colt added bitterly, "Whatever the hell that means."

"What jar?"

"A jar with no lid." An edge crept into his voice. "I've been over all of this with the experts and they all say either there's nothing there at all or else Peter set up some kind of trigger for releasing the memory he locked away—this jar with no lid he referred to."

"You're telling me there could be nothing inside your head at all? You could be dragging me all over the West Coast on a wild-goose chase?"

"There's something in my head. I'm sure of it." McQuade's eyes closed, almost like he was praying for it to be so.

What trouble had Peter laid on her doorstep *now?* Exactly how dangerous were those men tracking her and Colt? If McQuade was afraid of them, she probably ought to be fainting dead away with terror.


Colt started to reach up to lay a comforting hand on Layla's cheek, but something jerked sharply at his wrists. Something unpleasant stabbed at his gut. Fear, dammit. He yanked against the restraints, hearing the telltale rattle of metal. Handcuffs. Abruptly, memory engaged. Layla. Afraid of him. He'd offered to wear cuffs to calm her down. *Must've fallen asleep in the damned things.* Dreamed of Khan...

Lingering panic at being tied and helpless rippled through him. The shrinks said he might have a phobia of being tied up for the rest of his life. He hated this weakness in himself. He wanted to be back the way he was before he'd been captured and tortured within an inch of his sanity and his life.

"For the love of God, get these cuffs off me," he gritted out.

Terror was building in his gut like construction foam,

expanding into every crack in his soul. Puffing up, pushing out, suffocating him, insidious and unstoppable. Harsh breathing rasped in his ear and he realized with dismay that it was him making that awful gasping noise.

Layla reached for his face, cradling his cheeks with impossibly soft palms. "Easy, Colt. It'll be okay. Where's the key?"

"Dunno," he choked out. "Pocket."

She reached for his chest. Her hands slid inside his crumpled suit coat, warm and tentative through the thin fabric of his dress shirt. She fished around in the breast pocket before sliding her hands lower. As her fingers trailed across his stomach, every muscle there knotted in a tight washboard of pleasure. She leaned over him to check the lower pockets of his jacket, and the tempting swell of a breast loomed in front of him again. An urge to raise his head, to suckle the nipple pushing impudently at her silk blouse, nearly overcame him. Geez. He was totally losing it. But hey. She'd momentarily distracted him from his panic attack.

Of course, as soon as he thought of it, the damned thing came roaring back full force. And with it came a large dose of humiliation that she was seeing him in this state. He was supposed to be strong. In control. Able to handle anything. But he couldn't even stop himself from hyperventilating at the moment.

"I can't find the key," she said worriedly.

"Pants," he mumbled.

"Great," she griped under her breath. She sounded nearly as uncomfortable as he felt.

He must distract himself or he was going to do something really stupid like faint. He focused on her chest looming inches from his face as she contorted herself searching for the missing key.

She either wasn't wearing a bra, or the one she had on was damned flimsy, given how clearly he saw the outline of her chest under her blouse. He did his best not to imagine the creamy fullness or tight, pink nipples pushing against white lace, but with them all but brushing against his face, it was damned hard not to.

Her hand slid into the front pocket of his slacks. Parts of him perilously close to her fingers leaped to eager attention. *Oh, for crying out loud.* He gritted his teeth and silently begged her to find the damned key before he completely embarrassed himself on top of everything else. At least he was breathing deeply now.

She tugged on his sleeve, and he rolled obediently to his side. His shoulder protested, but he ignored the ice picks stabbing the joint. His abrupt discomfort elsewhere was much more distracting. He stifled a groan as her hand slid into his other front pocket and fished around. She didn't find the key, but she found something else that made her cheeks flame as hot as his and made his discomfort even worse.

She mumbled, "Key's not there."

He rolled onto his stomach, grateful for the modicum of privacy it afforded him. "Back pocket," he grunted.

Of course, it was in the last pocket she checked. She had thoroughly fondled his rear end before the damned key showed up. In fact, he was getting panicky again by the time she fumbled at his wrists. "Stay still," she ordered.

The instant the lock popped free he rolled over and sat up. Layla lurched, but not fast enough. He banged into her hard enough he nearly knocked her backward off the bed. He grabbed her shoulders quickly and dragged her upright. Which also had the effect of plastering her body against his.

A world of sensation flooded him, as sweetly intoxicating as the memories of Khan had been agonizing. She was soft. And warm. And pliable. Vulnerable. And dammit, all of a sudden she was breathing as hard as he was.

Their gazes met. Hers was confused, darkening with passion. His had to be just as confused. Lord knew what else she saw in his eyes.

Sure, he'd had women since he got back from his captivity. But that had been sex for the sake of sex. Mostly, they'd been women who'd gotten off on the idea of healing the wounded hero. One step up from the usual groupies who hung around military bases looking for Special Forces soldiers to hook up with. None of them had fired his blood like this woman had…this woman he was supposed to *work* with to figure out what the hell Peter Morrison had done to him. A woman he had no business thinking of in *that* way.

As if his worry about it conjured the thought in her head, she had to go and touch him just then. He became aware of her hands soft on his chest, drifting up his arms and across his shoulders, flitting feather-light along his jaw, tracing his brow.

"Are you all right?" she whispered in what sounded like genuine concern. "You're not going to freak out on me again now that you're awake, are you?"

"No. I won't mistake you for Khan now that I'm awake."

"Do I want to know who Khan is?"

"He's the bastard who killed Peter and nearly killed me."

"And you were dreaming about him? I'm so sorry."

"You've got nothing to apologize for. Trust me. Waking

up to see your face in front of me was the nicest sight I've seen since I got home."

She smiled brilliantly, about knocking him clean off the bed. "Really? You're not just saying that to be nice?"

"I don't remember how to do nice."

Her gaze faltered and fell away from his. "Of course. I'm sorry. For a moment there I thought you might... It was nothing. Wishful thinking..."

*Aww, hell.* He'd hurt her feelings. Or worse, scared her. He wasn't kidding. It had been years since he'd dealt with a woman's feelings. Since long before Kyrgyzstan. He was about as smooth as a pissed-off porcupine these days. He sighed and released her arms to cup her face carefully in his big hands. Her skin was delicious. All satin-and-white-chocolate smooth.

"Tell me what you were going to say, Layla."

Her hands drifted to his wrists but she made no move to pull his hands off her. And, God help him, he had no will to stop touching her.

"Please," he whispered, desperate all of a sudden to know her mind. Or maybe he was just desperate to make some sort of normal connection with another human being that didn't involve fear and torture and death.

"Well, uh, I sort of..." She took a deep breath. "For a minute there, I thought maybe you were attracted to me."

Was that all that was bothering her? He sagged in relief. "You thought right."

"Huh?"

"You're were right. I was...am...attracted to you. I was worried that I had scared you."

"You did when you were thrashing around and moaning. I've never heard such pain in someone's voice. I can't imagine what you were experiencing in your dream."

He gazed bleakly at her. "It wasn't my imagination. I was remembering." As dismay blossomed in her gaze, he added, "I'm sorry you had to see that."

"I don't mind—" She broke off. "Actually, I mind very much. No human being should have to suffer like that."

He shrugged. "It's part of the job."

"A job no one should have to do!" she declared indignantly.

He smiled. "I'm all for wars ending forever. But I doubt that's going to happen any time soon. Until then, men will continue committing atrocities against each other, and men trained like me will continue to be necessary to protect our national interests."

"No wonder you think you're going crazy if you have to haul all that pain around inside you."

He smiled reluctantly. "Hauling around Peter's little gift is worse."

She nodded sagely. "He could be a pain in the butt like that sometimes."

Frustration rolled through him, but he reminded himself that he was one step closer to solving the mystery of Peter's secret than he'd been before he met Layla.

He tried to smile his gratitude at her, but all that came to him was an inexplicable sadness that she'd had to see his private pain. No human being deserved to share what he'd been through. It was too much for him to bear, let alone some soft-hearted civilian with no training in how to deal with torture.

She murmured, "How can I make things better for you?"

He'd heard that line from women before, but none of them had sounded as genuinely upset as Layla. Of course, he hadn't ever been handcuffed and had a full-blown panic attack at being restrained in front of any of the others, either.

He smiled crookedly at her. "As tempting as it is to tell you how much I need comforting, I'm not the kind of jerk to take advantage of a woman's sympathy like that."

She stared at him for a moment that stretched out between them like a giant rubber band, growing tighter and tighter until it thrummed with tension. "But what if I want to comfort you?" she whispered.

The rubber band snapped back, slamming into him with a force that knocked the wind right out of him. He shook his head. "It wouldn't be right."

"Colt?" she murmured.

"Hmm?"

"You talk too much."

He laughed. That was a first. Most women accused him of being the worst sort of strong, silent male. But then her mouth was on his, all butter soft and sugar sweet, and any thought of laughter evaporated off him like water droplets on a hot griddle. Steam heat built crazily in his gut as her lips parted against his stunned ones. Her tongue traced the outline of his mouth. And then, somebody save him, she made a sound in the back of her throat that was part moan, part demand and part pure, freaking heaven.

His arms swept around her, drawing her against him as he fell back onto the bed, taking her with him. She was tinier than he'd realized as she sprawled across his big body. "We really shouldn't—" he started.

"Colt?"

"Yes?"

"Hush up."

He chuckled as the buttons of his shirt fell open beneath her clever fingers and then—ahh, yes—her hands roamed across his chest. If she didn't quit making that little sound like the best-tasting treat on the planet was melting on her tongue, he was going to lose what little sanity he had left.

Her thigh pressed against the junction of his legs, her belly molding to his stomach as if she'd been made for him. His shirt fell completely open, and her silk blouse provided more titillation than coverage against his skin.

"Honey, if you don't stop this—"

Her fingers touched his mouth and she rose up over him, his own personal angel, glowing brighter than the sun for him. She spoke gently. "If I do stop this, I'll wonder for the rest of my life what could've been. I've lived with more than my share of regrets, and I imagine you have, too."

He had to give her that one. He'd had all the time in the world while he was imprisoned to examine his life and figure exactly how and where he'd screwed up.

She gazed deep into his eyes, pinning him in place more firmly than any handcuffs ever had. "I don't want to regret this, so I'd appreciate it if you would quit trying to be a gentleman and kiss me back, please."

What could he do? The lady'd said please. Without further ado, he surrendered to his very own Valentine angel. He surged up, rolling her over until she lay beneath him, ready and willing to save his soul. He stroked her hair back, running his fingers through the spun gold. It flowed like water over his hands. He kissed her eyebrows, her jaw, the perfect column of her neck. And then he slipped his hand behind her neck, lifted her to him and kissed her.

Leaning on one elbow, he came up for air long enough to trail his fingers down her body, eliciting another one of those intoxicating sighs of hers. He reached for the hem of her blouse, easing it upward, slowly revealing the snowy flesh of her torso. The edge of a transparent black bra came into view. Not white lace, after all. Sexy black, instead. His angel had a naughty streak, did she? Exultation erupted in his gut at this discovery. He cupped her breast, molding its resilience with his fingers and relishing the way she arched up into his touch.

A jangling noise startled him badly, and Layla's eyes flew open as she lurched against him. Murder exploded in his gut at the interruption before his brain belatedly kicked in. *Telephone.* The device sitting on the nightstand jangled again. He reached across Layla and picked up the receiver. He glanced at the alarm clock beside the phone. Not quite 5:00 a.m.

"What?" he snarled into the phone.

"Two men just came and asked about you. They had a picture of you. I told them like you asked me to that we didn't have any guests matching your description."

Colt swore luridly under his breath. "Have they gone?"

"Yes. They drove out of the parking lot a minute ago. I waited until they were gone to call like you said."

"Good fellow. I owe you another hundred bucks for your help." He hung up the receiver and looked down at Layla, still sprawled beneath him, more tempting than could possibly be legal. He swore again. "I'm sorry, honey. We've got to go."

"Now?" she asked plaintively.

He smiled at the regret in her voice. He knew the feeling. "Unfortunately, yes." He ought to feel relieved. He undoubtedly had just dodged making a huge mistake with her. But instead he felt like putting his fist through a wall.

He wiped down the room for fingerprints while Layla sat on the edge of the bed and watched him glumly. He made her stay behind him as they passed through the hotel lobby. He paused only long enough to palm a hundred-dollar bill to the clerk who'd saved their bacon, and then they slipped into the shadows of the parking lot. Layla was silent behind him while he scanned the area for hostiles.

When he was positive their followers were indeed gone, he led her to his rental car. Avoiding major highways, he guided the car north as the sky turned gray, and then pink in the east. Layla was quiet and thoughtful, but he was afraid to ask her what she was thinking now that the bald light of day had banished last night's strange magic.

It was midmorning and he'd just finished refueling the car before she finally roused herself and spoke. "Where are we going?"

"To Sturgeon's Corners."

"Aww, crap," Layla breathed.

# Chapter 3

As familiar buildings and streets began to pass outside the window, Layla rolled her eyes. "God, I hate this town."

"So did Peter," Colt answered her grimly. "But it's the logical place to start looking for this supposed jar trigger of his, don't you think?"

She frowned. "Won't the bad guys arrive at the same conclusion?"

He shrugged. "It's not like I've got any choice. I've got to find his trigger and get Peter's secret out of my head before he takes me over completely."

"Whoa. Takes you over?" she exclaimed. "You think he did more to you than just plant a hypnotic suggestion?"

Colt threw her a dark look from the driver's seat. "I think I might actually go a little crazy if I don't get this thing out of my head," he mumbled. "The dreams are getting worse. Peter's in them all, and he keeps telling me to find the trigger. It's getting creepy."

She turned in the seat to stare at him. "I've never heard of dreams making anyone nuts, but I believe you. Seriously, Colt, you need to get professional help with this. I'm a photographer, for goodness' sake. I have no experience with anything like this."

"The pros couldn't help. They don't know anything about Peter Morrison. Everyone pretty much agrees that, until we figure out how and where he hid the trigger, I'm hosed."

She stared at him in dismay. No wonder the guy was having massive nightmares. "What do you expect me to do about your problem?" she finally asked.

"I need you to tell me everything you know about Peter. What's the significance of a jar to him?"

"You do realize I know an awful lot about him, right? It could take me days to tell you everything."

He snorted. "It took him *months* to tell me everything he knew about you."

She winced at that. She could only imagine some of the humiliating things this total stranger knew about her. Although, after last night's passionate exchange, maybe not so total a stranger. And she had to admit, after her near miss with seducing Colt, she was in much less of a hurry to escape his magnetic charm. He'd been right, of course. Under the circumstances, it would've been a bad idea for them to make love. Darn it.

"Do you have anything specific in mind to try once we get to Sturgeon's Corners?" she asked reluctantly.

He shrugged. "I thought we could check out the places you and Peter used to hang out. See if anything triggers a memory in you about him. I have the feeling we're looking for a single reference. Something he figured you'd remember."

She frowned, wracking her brain to no avail. What was she missing? Nothing whatsoever came to mind regarding Peter and jars. No significant memories, no funny moments, nothing that would've stuck in her memory. Darn him! Why did he have to be such a puzzle freak? He'd known just how much she hated riddles and brain teasers. Did he have to go and leave one last puzzle to torture her like this? And, oh by the way, leave some sexy hunk's sanity hanging in the balance? Frankly, it sounded like a very bad joke, Peter style.

"Are you sure this isn't just Peter pulling your leg from beyond the grave? It wouldn't be entirely out of keeping with his personality to pull this inappropriate a stunt."

Colt shoved a hand through his short hair, standing it up on end so sexily she had to look away before she threw herself on the man driving the car down the highway at seventy miles per hour.

"I wondered that until people started trying to kill me. They believe Peter put something important in my head. Important enough to kill for."

"Why would they believe that?"

"Pete was a brilliant scientist. Who knows what he said under torture? He might have talked about something he was working on for the government, or some invention he'd come up with. Believe me, I wish I knew."

She replied, "Well, Peter never talked to me about his work. He'd drop one technical phrase and I'd zone out."

"God, this is weird," he muttered.

"We'll figure it out," she replied.

Colt turned left at the next stoplight and she grimaced as she realized where he was going. Peter's house. The neat, craftsman bungalow was a different color than when she'd last seen it, and someone had added river rock cladding to the square pillars holding up the front porch. But beyond that, it looked the same.

Colt parked the car across the street and turned off the engine. She watched him warily as he stared at her looking at the house.

"Anything?" he murmured.

She frowned. "No. And that doesn't surprise me. This is the last place Peter would send anyone he remotely cared about."

"Why did Peter hate his parents so much? I mean, I know they didn't accept him and thought he was…strange. But they were his folks."

"He didn't hate them. He just wanted them to love him a little. He didn't even need them to accept his oddities. But they never did give him the love he craved. They merely counted the years until they could get rid of him. At best, they called him an embarrassment. At worst, they declared him an abomination."

Colt frowned. "Pete never told me that."

"Guess he had a few secrets from you after all," she commented. A spark of hope lit in her gut that maybe Peter hadn't totally humiliated her before this man after all. But the next place Colt drove the car thoroughly dispelled that notion.

She looked out over Sturgeon's Corners from the scenic overview that also served as Lovers' Lane for the local teen population. Most people would call the town a quaint fishing village. She just saw her painfully awkward youth and years of desperation to escape a place she had never fit in. This particular spot was also the site of the most embarrassing moment of her entire life.

She and Peter had both been sixteen and a little drunk from the six-pack of beer and a couple of joints they'd shared up here one sultry summer night. That was the night they decided it was time to lose their respective virginities. It had never occurred to her to give hers to anyone else. She'd loved Peter since the first grade. Of course her first boy would be him.

They'd giggled a lot while they struggled to get partially undressed in the back of his father's Buick. And then there'd been the issue of figuring out where the extra elbow and odd knee was supposed to go. And then Peter had been fumbling between them and there'd been more laughter. And then a flash of fiery pain that had pierced her foggy mind. And then…

She glanced over at Colt, who stared grimly out the windshield of the car, resolutely not looking over at her. Sick knowing washed over her. *He knew.* Her cheeks flamed and an overwhelming urge to crawl under the front seat nearly overcame her. She briefly considered jumping out of the car and fleeing. But Colt would just come after her and drag her back here to pile disgrace on top of humiliation. She closed her eyes in a failed attempt to gather some calm to herself.

Her voice thick with shame, she asked, "Do you know what this place is?"

"Yup."

"Did Peter—" Her voice broke. She couldn't even bring herself to say the words aloud.

Colt answered her unspoken question heavily. "Yeah. He told me."

Her stomach dropped like a lead brick, taking the last shreds of her dignity with it. She turned away, pressing her forehead against the cold glass of the window. Her face surely had burst into fire, it felt so painfully hot. She mumbled, "I'd kill him if he weren't already dead."

"I'm sorry." Colt's voice was grim. "I thought maybe

this place would trigger some important memory—" He broke off.

Oh, it had triggered a major memory all right. One she'd give a whole lot to forget.

The same wind as fifteen years ago blew mournfully through the towering pine trees. The same sense of unreality flowed over her. The memory of Peter freezing above her moments after deflowering her, of him staring down at her in dawning dismay, filled her mind.

*"What's wrong, Peter?"*

*"You're all…wet. And…squishy soft."*

*Epic embarrassment flared in her. "Well…yeah. I'm a girl. That's how we're made."*

*And then he slid out of her, sitting up and turning away in the dark. He stared out the window for a long time. Long enough for her to scramble away and put her clothes right. Long enough for a single tear to slide millimeter by millimeter all the way from the corner of her eye to her chin, tremble there for a while, and finally drop onto her tightly clenched fingers.*

*"Is something wrong with me?" she eventually whispered.*

*"No! It's not you. I think…I think…" He paused a long time, then, "I think…I'm gay."*

She'd stared at his averted profile that night, shocked to hear the words. Although, in retrospect, the signs had been there all along. She'd challenged the assertion, of course, declaring that it was just the shock of having sex for the first time that had made it feel weird to him. But when he'd reluctantly confessed that what he'd really wanted to do was flip her over—or better, have someone do the same to him—she gave up trying to talk him out of being gay.

Everything and nothing had changed between them

after that night. She'd given up on her childhood fantasy of marrying him, having his children and living happily ever after with him anywhere but Sturgeon's Corners. In some ways, their friendship had strengthened with that one last secret erased between them. Peter had loved her for accepting him as he was—a feat his parents never accomplished. She'd loved him more like a brother after that. But it had also signaled the beginning of Peter's emotional withdrawal deep into himself, something from which he'd never really emerged.

"God, I miss Peter," she whispered aloud, but mostly to herself.

"I miss him, too."

She glanced over at Colt. He seemed an unlikely companion for cynical, sarcastic, out-of-the-closet Peter.

Colt shrugged. "We went to hell and back together. That's a bond not too many people ever have to share. He was there for me through some rough times."

She had a hard time imagining times rough enough to make this strong, silent warrior that desperate for companionship. Not that Peter had been a bad guy at heart. The two men were just so…different.

"Did Peter like you?" she asked.

Colt considered the question thoughtfully. "Yeah. I think he did. He used to hassle me about being smarter than the average marine. I kept trying to explain to him that I'm in the army, and marines are attached to the navy, but he never got it."

She smiled reluctantly. "Peter was a smart cookie. He got it. He was just giving you heck."

Colt smiled back. "I knew that. It was just a thing we did to make us smile in a place where smiles were hard to come by."

They sat in silence for a while and looked down over the small fishing village heading home for dinner after a long day's work.

She asked reflectively, "What do you suppose Peter came up with if his big secret is some new scientific breakthrough?"

"I haven't the slightest idea. I know he worked on missile defense systems. But that's about it. He couldn't risk talking about his work with me in case our prison cells were bugged."

She shuddered. "How did you survive that? Paranoia would have made me crazy."

Colt's gaze, suddenly a molten shade of golden brown, speared into her. "I thought about women to distract myself." His sudden grin flashed white in the dark car interior. "I imagine Peter thought about men."

"Did you miss—" She broke off. She'd kissed the guy and felt his reaction to her. Of course he'd missed women.

"Did I miss sex? I missed decent food and hot showers and real beds. I craved sex. I must be losing my touch with the ladies if you had to ask that after our kiss last night."

Jeez, she was a dork. Of course the guy had missed sex. What man—what *human*—wouldn't miss the affection and closeness, not to mention the raw pleasure? Memory of the way Colt had all but devoured her with eyes and mouth and hands was vivid in her mind. So, he'd been thinking about that kiss today, too, huh?

"Your touch is just fine," she blurted.

His mouth quirked up into a smile. "Good to know I haven't completely lost it."

He stared outside for a long time. Long enough for the sun to set in a blaze of orange and red and for twilight

to settle around them. Long enough for her to get bored
and for her mind to drift entirely of its own volition back
to their steamy encounter in the hotel room last night.
Anticipation of the coming night even had time to build
low in her belly. Lord, she was a mess. She was lusting
after a stranger now.

Except he was rapidly becoming something other
than a stranger. It had to be hard for him to show her
his weakness like this. To talk about his prisoner-of-war
experience. He didn't strike her as the kind of man who
relished wallowing in his emotions. But he was forcing
himself to do just that as he took her on this trip to her
and Peter's past.

How much about her did Colt already know? Besides
whatever Peter'd told him, he already knew that she didn't
mind long silences in a car, and that she'd hated growing
up here, and that she loved to be kissed while he played
with more sensitive parts of her anatomy....

She broke off *that* train of thought irritably. "Have you
got any more intensely unpleasant trips down memory
lane to throw at me tonight?" she asked in resignation.

He glanced sidelong at her. "I really am sorry about
bringing you up here. It was nothing personal—" He
winced. "Bad choice of words. Sorry."

She sighed. "It's unnerving to realize that you know
such private things about me and I know nothing about
you." She left the statement hanging leadingly.

He threw her a sidelong look that might have been
alarm or amusement. Either way he retorted, "What? You
want me to tell you about the first time I had sex to even
the score or something?"

It sounded dumb when he said the words aloud. She
shrugged and started to turn away, but his large hand

landed on her shoulder and dragged her back around to face him.

He sighed. "Her name was Kristen and she was a cheerleader. She was seventeen and I was fifteen. We did it in a car, too." He glanced around the interior of the Prius. "It was a tighter fit than this. I think, in here, if I leaned the seat back you could sit on my lap reasonably comfortably—"

An image of straddling him and riding him to oblivion exploded across her mind. Liquid heat pulsed between her legs, startling her badly. She was not an intensely sexual person, thank you very much.

He continued, "That girl was insatiable. We went at it for hours before she finally let me take a break. Of course the first several times I didn't last more than a few minutes—" He broke off. "Sorry. Oversharing."

Several? Her mind reeled at the concept. Dang.

"Are you all right, Layla? You look strange."

"Uhh, I'm okay," she replied breathlessly. Good grief. What was wrong with her voice?

"Will you let me help erase the painful memories this place holds and replace them with a good one?"

She nodded mutely and he leaned across the gear shift to hug her. His mouth was so close to hers she couldn't form a coherent thought.

"It's my fault I dredged up the bad stuff by bringing you back here," he murmured deliciously against her lips. "My job to fix the problem, don't you think?"

How her arms wound up around his neck, and she ended up in his lap, her thigh thrown across his hips, the steering wheel jabbing her in the lower back and the gear shift jabbing her left leg, she wasn't really sure. And then, shockingly, there were no extra elbows or awkward legs. Just the bulging heat of him rubbing against equally hot and throbbing parts of her, and his mouth moving across hers, his tongue laving hers with the most incredible results.

She arched her back—purely to escape the steering wheel, of course. It had nothing to do with thrusting her aching breasts forward for his attention. His mouth and clever fingers were dragging across her fabric-clad nipples, easing the ache and creating an even more driving need deep within her.

"If it makes you feel better," he murmured around the tight pucker of her flesh in his mouth, "Peter never said anything to me about what a great kisser you are. Or about how sexy you are."

Laughter bubbled up within her. "I highly doubt he noticed."

"Well, honey, I've noticed. I like everything I see. And taste. And touch." And then his hands were sliding up under her skirt, which had bunched around her hips without her noticing it. She gasped as he worked his magic on her, all the while holding her gaze hypnotically and smiling into her eyes.

A shimmering ball of energy began to wind tighter and tighter within her belly and she struggled to focus on Colt's gaze. His finger slid across the silky wash of flesh between her thighs. It felt tight and swollen and so sensitive she nearly screamed when he circled it lazily with his fingertip. And then a large, blunt finger intruded into the core of the volcano building within her. Her feminine muscles spasmed and Colt surprised her by groaning along with her. His finger slid deeper, retreated, and then went deeper still. Her head fell forward to rest upon his solid shoulder as she quivered from head to foot. What was he doing to her?

"Want me to stop?" he whispered.

"No," she groaned.

His teeth closed on her earlobe and his fingers plunged hard and fast into her wet heat, stretching her and filling her as every bone in her body commenced melting. The heel of his palm rocked against her swollen flesh until she thought she would die with pleasure.

She hung on to him for dear life and…surrendered. That was the only word for it. For the second time in her life, she gave her body over without reservation to a man. Same place. Same setting. But, oh, how incredibly different the outcome. Replacing bad memories indeed. He'd blown them sky-high.

The ball of energy finally filled her so brilliantly she couldn't see, let alone breathe. And then, without warning, it exploded into a million pieces, ripping through her like molten shrapnel. She literally felt shredded by the excess of pleasure that tore through her. She cried out and Colt's mouth was there to capture her joy, drinking it greedily into himself.

She collapsed on top of him, and he didn't seem to mind. His strong arms held her close while she shuddered out the aftermath of the most amazing orgasm—heck, maybe the first true orgasm—she'd ever experienced. After a few minutes, as her pulse finally came back down into the realm of sane, he murmured, "Again?"

"Really?"

"Honey, I could watch you do that all night long. And unlike your buddy, Peter, I'm not going anywhere until you tell me to."

Abruptly, she realized his fingers were still seated deep within her. And that her swollen flesh, which was suddenly clenched tight around those fingers, was—if possible— even more sensitive than it had been a few minutes ago.

Of their own volition, her hips rocked forward. "Oh," she breathed.

This time she took the lead, self-consciousness forgotten, impaling herself upon his hand with abandon. "That's it," he urged. "Show me what you like."

Somewhere en route to driving herself over the edge into oblivion once more, it occurred to her that she would never think of this place again without something wonderful unfurling deep within her. Fixing memories? Heck, he'd fixed something in her soul.

She came apart at least as violently as before. This time he nudged her chin up with his free hand and insisted she keep her eyes open as the pleasure began to break over her. It was so intimate she could hardly wrap her mind around gazing deep into his eyes as she shattered for him.

The moment of perfection stretched out, hanging around them both in suspended animation as they went utterly still, staring into each other's naked souls. And maybe that was why they both heard the twig snap outside.

## Chapter 4

Colt swore under his breath as he unceremoniously dumped Layla off his lap. He'd heard enough twigs snap in his life to know without a shadow of a doubt that the weight of a human had broken that branch. They'd found him and Layla.

"Get down," he ordered. He ducked as well, searching over the edge of the window frame outside for any sign of assailants. Damn. The bastards were too good for him to spot. "We've got to go," he muttered.

"So start the car and get out of here," she whispered back frantically.

A male voice shouted outside, "We're federal agents. Freeze, McQuade. We have you and your hostage surrounded. Come out of the car with your hands behind your head. Slowly. And don't even think about using the woman for cover. We have snipers."

The sniper thing might be a bluff, but then it might not

be, either. Not that it mattered. He would never put Layla in that kind of danger. Colt looked across the car at his terrified companion. Crap. She looked ready to cut and run.

He ordered her forcefully enough to penetrate her panic, "When I tell you to, open your door and slide out to the ground. Lie flat. I'll be right behind you. Ready?"

"No! I'm not ready! What the heck's going on? Who's out there? And why do you want me to—"

"Honey, you ask too many questions." He reached across her, opened the door and unceremoniously shoved her out. Her rump had no sooner hit the dirt than he rolled out after her, covering her body with his. She stared up at him, shocked.

"McQuade!" Swearing erupted behind them. "Get him!"

"Shh," he whispered to Layla. And then he wrapped his arms around her and started to roll, taking her with him.

"The cliff—" she started.

Lord, that woman could talk. He had no free hand to press over her mouth to silence her, so he did the only thing he could. He kissed her. And that was how they rolled off the precipice, mouths and bodies locked together.

Thankfully, Layla was too stunned by the abrupt drop to fight him as he contorted violently to shift them to a feetfirst position as they slid down the rocky slope. His back scraped and banged across the rocks painfully. But after Khan, pain was an entirely relative thing. Colt gritted his teeth together and took the beating as they bumped and bounced nearly a hundred feet down the steep incline with him acting as a human toboggan for Layla on top of him.

Their descent ended abruptly as they fetched up hard against a tree trunk. He grunted as his breath was mostly knocked out of him. He did his best to absorb the impact and protect Layla from harm.

"You okay?" he gasped as soon as he could breathe again.

"No!" she exclaimed under her breath. "What the—"

"Shh."

Thankfully, she obeyed him this time. He set her on her feet and climbed to his. The slope was still steep, but down here trees provided heavy cover from the men above. He led her by the hand, bracing on tree trunks whenever they threatened to lose control of their descent. They finally reached level ground, breathless and bruised.

"Well, that was fun," Layla panted.

"Can you run?" he asked tersely. They still were far from safe.

"Do I have a choice?" she retorted.

He flashed her a grin. "Nope."

They took off, heading into town. He spotted exactly what he needed a block ahead. A soft-top Jeep parked in front of a darkened house. Its doors were even unlocked. He ordered Layla to climb in while he ducked under the dashboard and went to work hot-wiring the vehicle. In under a minute the engine roared to life.

"You're stealing a car?" Layla squawked.

"Borrowing it." When she continued to stare at him accusingly, he added, "I'll pay for the repairs when I return it, if it'll make you feel better."

That seemed to mollify her. He guided the car north out of town.

"Are we safe?" she asked as Sturgeon's Corners retreated quickly into the night behind them. He was too busy watching the rearview mirror to answer her right away. And besides, he didn't know the answer. It didn't help that something wasn't sitting quite right in his gut. Their escape had been too damned easy. He drove a few more miles before the warning feeling got so strong he finally had to pull over.

"*Now* what?" Layla demanded.

At least she was back to asking questions one at a time. He replied, "I dunno. Gimme a sec."

He jumped out of the Jeep and moved around it slowly, running his hands up under the wheel wells and behind the bumpers. It wasn't until he lay on his back and peered up under the chassis that he spotted the tracking device. The Jeep had been a trap. And he'd taken the bait, hook, line and sinker. Swearing, he pulled the magnetically attached radio free. He looked around for somewhere to ditch the thing and heard the sound of running water. Perfect.

Colt rummaged around in the trash on the back floor of the vehicle and found a zipper-seal plastic bag. He dumped out the moldy sandwich and shoved the radio inside. "Back in a sec," he murmured to Layla. He jogged into the woods, following the sound of water. The stream was small but fast moving. He blew the bag full of air, sealed it tight and tossed it into the water. It bobbed out of sight in seconds.

If he was lucky, that would buy him and Layla enough time to lose their pursuers and figure out what the hell was going on. If they were lucky, they just might outrun whoever was chasing them. But he knew from experience that might be a big *if*.

Layla all but cried in relief when he climbed back in the Jeep. "Hey," he murmured. "I would never ditch you in the middle of a date."

She gave him a watery smile as he guided the car back out onto the road.

"Some Valentine's Day this is turning into," she sniffed.

"Next year. Dinner. On me. I'll even take you to some vegetarian joint. Some place nice with no bad guys chasing after us."

She smiled and dashed the tears off her cheeks. "You're on."

"Is there a boyfriend back in San Francisco I'm going to have to beat up to get my Valentine's date with you?"

"Hardly. I'm too square for most of the men there."

He laughed. "Then they're idiots." He meant it, too. She was every bit as sweet and funny and kind-hearted as Peter had said she was. And on top of it all, she was smoking-hot. Any man would be a fool not to hang on tight to a woman like her.

She threw him a grateful look.

He knew from Pete about how her parents had mostly abandoned her and her sisters as kids. And then, of course, there'd been Peter's abandonment of her when he'd gone away to work for the government. Pete had felt bad about that but had worried that if he didn't leave Layla she'd never emotionally connect with a man who could make her happy in every way. Apparently, Peter's fears for her had been well founded.

Colt drove grimly for close to an hour, wrestling with a decision. He hadn't wanted to do it, but with Layla's safety to consider, too, he had no choice. He had to involve his family in this mess. He and Layla needed to go to ground someplace where the team chasing him would have no idea to look for him. And for better or worse, he knew the perfect place.

His cousin had a place up on the Olympic Peninsula.

A little hunting cabin tucked way back in the woods. And Cousin Joe was the cussed type—didn't like people knowing his business. Both the land and the cabin were registered to a corporation in the Cayman Islands. Joe always said that when the world order went to hell, he was heading for the cabin and everyone else was on his own. From Colt's perspective, hell was already here.

He drove straight through, stopping only once to gas up and buy a few supplies at a gas station convenience store, including a package of underwear that would no doubt mortify Layla when she saw it. He knew Joe had probably stocked the cabin with nonperishable food.

Layla slept for much of the drive, which was just as well. It was best that she not know where he was taking them just in case the worst happened and the two of them got separated. The idea of being away from her was surprisingly disturbing to him. She gave him hope for fixing the mess inside his head that no one else had been able to give him. Not to mention, the lady was very easy on the eyes. Once, when Pete had been delirious with a fever, he'd raged at the fact that Layla couldn't become a man he could truly love. Having met her now, Colt was abjectly grateful that Peter's wish had never come true.

They pulled into the cabin in the wee hours of the night. He woke Layla and she stumbled into the cabin without much curiosity. He guided her to the one tiny bedroom and she fell into bed straightaway. He put away the groceries and went to check on her.

"Join me?" she mumbled as he tucked the covers up around her chin.

He stopped, staring down at her. "You need your rest."

"I'll sleep better with you close," she murmured.

Well, okay then. He kicked off his shoes, shrugged

out of his jacket and climbed into the narrow double bed beside her. Immediately, she rolled back against him, snuggling her bottom against him in a way guaranteed to make him not sleep for a long time to come. Sighing, he draped his arm over her waist and held her warmth close. She tangled her fingers in his and pulled his hand close to the resilience of her breast. It was tantalizing against his knuckles. At least he'd gotten some sleep last night, because he damned well wasn't going to get any tonight.

Layla woke up slowly. She was encased in a delicious cocoon of warmth and safety that lulled her into lingering in this place halfway between sleep and waking. Her mind drifted lazily, gradually working its way to yesterday's events and their panicked flight from the summit overlooking Sturgeon's Corners.

A tiny, annoying buzz of disquiet intruded upon her contentment. Slowly it took shape in her mind. Those men who'd surrounded their car had identified themselves as federal agents. They'd called her Colt's "hostage." Could it be true? Had he kidnapped her so cleverly that she didn't even realize she was his prisoner? Was he the bad guy after all? She popped abruptly to full consciousness.

Was it possible Colt had duped her? Was she so desperate she'd just thrown herself at the first sexy man ever to show a real interest in her? How was she supposed to know who was telling the truth—Colt or the men chasing him?

Oh, my gosh. That heavy blanket was no blanket at all. It was Colt's arm lying across her. And that was his torso pressed against the entire length of her back. Of course. If she were his hostage, he would need to sleep with her like this to make sure she didn't sneak away from him while he was unconscious!

Now what the heck was she supposed to do?

She had to escape. *Now.* She eased out from under his arm by achingly slow inches, determined to get far away from him before he woke. Finally, she was free of his arm and eased to her feet beside the bed. She glanced down at him and jolted as his brown eyes gazed steadily at her.

"Oh! I was trying not to wake you up," she mumbled, blushing. *Damn. Busted.*

"Bathroom's in there," he said, pointing at a closed door across the compact space.

Maybe it had a window she could climb out.

"Everything okay?" he asked.

"Uhh, yeah. Fine." Crap. He was suspicious. She'd have to wait for another moment to make her escape. "Where are we?" she asked.

"At a cabin. In the woods," he replied. "We're miles from civilization. No one will ever think to look for us here. You're completely safe."

*Completely trapped,* he meant. She cursed mentally. *Miles* from anyone else? So much for escaping. She trudged into the bathroom to take a shower and think up a new plan. If only someone knew where she was. Why, oh why, hadn't she told a friend about her dinner plans at The Pleasant Peasant? She had no idea if anyone even knew she was gone, let alone in trouble.

As she dressed in the sweat suit Colt had produced from a dresser drawer for her and left on the bed along with some women's underwear—God only knew where he'd gotten that!—the silence of this place, wherever it was, pressed down on her. Talk about isolation. If only Peter were here. He'd help her. He was really smart. He'd figure out how to get her out of this mess. But he was gone and she was on her own. The next time Colt fell asleep, she would have to make a point of being awake and not draped under his arm.

Energized by having a plan of attack, she headed for the main room and the mouthwatering scents wafting from it. The kitchen was tucked in the far corner of the space, and Colt stood in front of a stove shirtless, expertly flipping a pancake by tossing it up in the air. For a kidnapper, the man sure was handsome.

"Hungry?" he asked over his shoulder.

"Starving." Better build up her strength for the escape to come. Besides, she loved pancakes. She heard the sizzle of meat frying on the stove, and the scent was appetizing enough to make a girl reconsider being vegetarian. "That sausage smells amazing."

"It's venison. I shot a buck two summers ago and my cousin had it made up into sausage and froze it. This is some of the last of it."

"You killed Bambi?" she exclaimed in horror. "And now you're going to *eat* him?"

He grinned at her as he set two plates down on the table. "Guilty as charged. I'm a born-again carnivore, honey."

Thankfully, her plate held only pancakes and no sign of sage-seasoned Bambi. She caught a whiff of real maple syrup and dug into the flapjacks with renewed enthusiasm.

"In a hurry?" he murmured.

She glanced up, startled. "Oh. Uh, yes. I want to get going on trying to figure out Peter's puzzle."

"I really do appreciate your help, Layla."

Polite for a kidnapper, he was. And Lord knew, the man kissed like a god—she broke off that train of thought sharply. He could very well be the enemy. She mustn't forget that.

Colt pushed back his plate. He'd eaten as quickly as she had. "Any ideas on what your buddy was up to?" he asked.

"He always loved games. Chess. Bridge. Backgammon. Anything that pitted his mind against other people's in direct competition. He'd even get all hyped up by a game of gin rummy."

Colt shrugged. "You're the expert on the guy." He cleared the table, and then sat down across from her once more. She tried not to get flustered at the way Colt's strong fingers riffled through the cards, nimble and clever. *Enemy, Layla. Enemy.*

She amended. *Hot enemy.*

The relatively simple gin rummy gave her time she desperately needed to think. She needed to let someone know where she was. That she needed a rescue. First time she was alone again, she would have to give her cell phone a try. It was the same cell phone Peter had declared a piece of crap four years ago. For once she regretted not having the latest in high-tech gadgetry. Her phone just had to work out here. She remembered hearing something about some cell phones having a GPS function that police could use to triangulate a phone's location.

She considered trying her phone in the tiny bathroom, but Colt would hear her talking for sure and flee with her before help could get here. Instead, she made a giant pot of soup for lunch and urged Colt to eat heartily. Sure enough, about an hour after he ate, he yawned widely.

"Why don't you lie down and take a nap?" she suggested. "I'll grab one of the books off the shelf and read a little. You could probably use a mental break from everything."

He nodded. "I suppose I could use a little shut-eye at that. Didn't sleep much last night—"

Uh-huh. He'd been guarding her. Making sure she didn't take off on him. She swore under her breath. So he *was* a kidnapper after all! She waited impatiently while he stretched out on the couch and fell asleep. But finally, he settled into a light snore. Time to go.

She stepped outside. The cabin sat slightly above a small valley cut in half by a pretty little stream. Massive walls of granite towered in every direction. She briefly considered trying to hike out of here. But she calculated her odds of getting lost to be approximately one hundred percent.

She flipped open her cell phone and wasn't surprised when she had no coverage. She would have to get to higher ground. She examined Mount Olympus and its neighbors until she decided which one looked the least steep and formidable. Navigating turned out to be surprisingly easy. She simply headed up. She consoled herself with the thought that the way back to the cabin would be equally simple—it was down.

She climbed the steep slope for perhaps a half hour. She had to be getting close to the summit. She panted for breath and her legs felt as if they were being slow roasted over a fire.

Time to try the phone again. Nothing. Still no signal.

She walked on, trudging up the mountain in between rest stops to catch her breath. The forest ended abruptly and granite outcroppings poked up all around her. It was a short walk to the summit after that. She hugged her arms across her chest as a sharp breeze cut through her sweatshirt.

"Okay, kid," she told herself. "Time to call in the cavalry."

She pulled out the phone and pushed the green telephone icon on its glowing face. She got a scratchy dial tone. She dialed and a male voice said, "9-1-1."

"Hello, I've been kidnapped and I'm on top of a mountain and I don't know where I am."

"Ma'am…can't understand…say again…"

*Damn!* He was breaking up terribly. "I've been kidnapped," she said slowly and loudly.

"Can't…" The line went dead.

"I lost him!" she wailed.

She walked all over the mountain top trying to get decent coverage, but always, a connection was tantalizingly just out of reach. Finally, as the battery was starting run down on her phone, she sat down dejected. She was never getting out of here.

She would die hungry and cold and alone. Was this what Peter had felt like when his time came? She felt rotten that she hadn't been with him when he died. She'd always imagined somehow that she would be with him at the end. At least Colt had been with him. The guy might be a psycho and a cleverly charming kidnapper, but any human company at the end for Peter had to have better than this awful solitude. Maybe Colt would find her in time to be with her when she died, too. It would be poetic irony.

She had to quit feeling sorry for herself and think. If she brought a mirror up here she might be able to signal an airliner. But she would need a sunny day for that. She glanced up at the heavy blanket of gray overhead. No chance of that today.

No way was she going back to that cabin and pretending to be all sweetness and light with Colt. She wasn't that good an actress. Particularly after they'd come so close to what, in retrospect, truly would have been a disaster.

And to think Valentine's Day was tomorrow. She'd gone from possible hot romance to colossal mess in a single day. That had to be a new record for her.

What would Peter say if he were here? He always had known how to make her feel better…or at least make her laugh. He would've made some snarky comment about having warned her that Valentine's Day romances were all a big hoax. And then he'd have teased her about her proclivity for giving away her virtue to every guy who took her to Lovers' Lane.

She rolled her eyes out of general principles. And what would Peter tell her about her current predicament? Knowing him, he'd make some cynical comment about not everyone who worked for Uncle Sam being a good guy. Maybe those federal agents—and she didn't even know for sure they really were federal agents—were the bad guys, after all. Maybe they'd said that stuff about her being Colt's hostage just to mess her up and get her to stop helping him.

"Thanks, Peter, wherever you are. Now I'm really confused!" she exclaimed to the rocks and sky around her.

A strange metallic pinging noise rang off the rock behind her. A chunk of granite hit her in the back and, panicked, she dived to the ground. What was that? Two more pings sounded and chips of granite flew, making her flinch anew. *Oh, my God.* Someone was *shooting* at her!

But who? Colt? Or the men chasing Colt?

## Chapter 5

Holy cow. What did she do now? Clearly, she needed to get off this mountaintop. But which direction? She wasn't qualified to make these sorts of life-and-death decisions. She looked around frantically. She probably needed to get away from this open space and into the trees so she could hide. One thing she knew for sure. If this wasn't Colt shooting at her, he was going to kill her himself when he caught up with her for exposing herself to danger like this.

She took a deep breath and headed off to her left. No bullets seemed to be coming from that direction. Not that she was in any way sure about that. She slithered along painfully on her belly, pausing every few yards to catch her breath. Maybe if she stood and pointed her finger at them like she had a gun they'd run away. Not.

Funny how, in the midst of flying bullets and eating dirt and praying for the trees to come closer, her mind seemed to be working with perfect clarity. As if it had detached itself from her body and the insanity going on around her. She reached the first bush, a scraggly little thing, but better than no cover at all.

A massive, dark shape flew at her out of nowhere, so fast she didn't even have time to make a sound before it landed on top of her, smashing all the breath out of her.

"You hit?" Colt growled in her ear.

"You mean by a bullet? No."

Three more shots rang out. *But Colt was lying on top of her.*

"I guess that means you're not the shooter, huh?" she mumbled.

"You thought I was shooting at you? Why on earth would I do that?"

She started to answer but he cut her off in an irritated whisper. "Never mind. Tell me later. If we live."

*If?* Great.

"Based on the trajectory of the last three shots, I'd say we're surrounded," he announced under his breath.

"What do we do now?" she whispered, panicked.

"You stay put. I'll go take out one of the shooters and make an opening to get you out of here."

"Just like that?" she asked incredulously.

He rolled his eyes. "I may be a head case, but I still know how to do my job."

"What if they know how to do theirs, too?" she retorted frantically.

"Then may the best man win. If I die, all of this will be moot anyway."

Lovely. He melted away into the scrub, leaving her alone with only her scrawny, little bush for comfort. She cast her mind back to every military movie she'd ever watched—and exactly none came to mind. She did remember television soldiers smearing their faces with mud and crushed leaves, though. And mimicking them gave her something to do that didn't involve running around like a panicked chicken and getting her head cut off.

She finished the impromptu mud facial and strained to hear something, anything to give her a clue as to what was happening out there. Seconds ticked by, and with the passage of each ominously silent minute her tension mounted. Was Colt alive? Had they captured him? Dragged him off to some secret lab to rip Peter's secrets out of his brain? Was she on her own out here in the middle of nowhere?

It felt like hours had passed but her rational mind said it had only been a few minutes. Did she trust him to protect her? Would he use her as a decoy to hold their attackers here while he snuck away and abandoned her? Somehow that didn't seem his style. Even if she was his hostage, she doubted he would let her go that easily. He'd be the possessive type—as a lover or as a kidnapper.

An apparition rose up practically right in front of her, and she drew breath to scream her head off, but Colt slapped a hand over her mouth again. Dang, he was fast.

"Let's go," he ordered under his breath.

He turned and raced into the woods, and she stumbled out from behind the little bush, following him as best she could. When she fell behind, he dropped back, took her right arm and bodily lifted her into a faster pace beside him. If someone didn't shoot them, she was surely going to fall and break her neck at this rate.

Without warning, he screeched to a stop and yanked her down beside him.

"What?" she whispered.

He pressed his finger to his lips by way of answer.

She glanced around nervously. Was one of the bad guys close, then? How close? If she wasn't mistaken, the daylight was going dimmer by the minute. Either the sun set a lot earlier than she realized, wherever they were, or bad weather was blowing in.

Neither prospect sounded that great.

After a few all-too-short minutes, Colt murmured, "Let's get moving. I want to get off this mountain before it rains and we get soaked."

As if his words were the signal for it, the skies opened up in a cold, drenching downpour that reduced visibility to a few yards. If nothing else, it washed the mud off her face, which had started to dry and was becoming uncomfortable.

"This weather is your fault," she grumbled at Colt as they moved along in the deepening gloom. "You had to go and mention rain."

"This rain is good. It'll mask both sounds and tracks."

She snorted. "And give us both our death of pneumonia."

"Nah. You're made of tougher stuff than that. And I've been in a lot worse conditions than this and not gotten sick."

She was grateful when he chose a route down the mountain, but it was still rough going. She'd be glad to get back on level ground again. Heck, she'd be really glad to get back to her regularly scheduled life and never hike all over a mountain again.

As they trekked on, she contemplated what she was going to tell Colt when he got around to asking what the heck she'd been doing on top of the mountain. As uncomfortable as it might be, she supposed she was better off to just stick with the truth. But in the meantime, maybe she could distract him.

She asked, "What do you intend to do once you figure out what Peter hid inside your head?"

He shrugged. "Depends on what it is, I suppose."

"What do you think the big secret is?"

He glanced over his shoulder at her. "Some sort of discovery or invention having to do with future weapon systems for the Department of Defense."

"Okay, let's say that's what Peter invented. What will you do with it?"

Colt answered heavily, "Hand it over to the right people."

"And who are they?"

"Hell if I know at this point. I've got gun-toting killers claiming to be from the U.S. government trying to kill me, and foreign mafia bosses offering me sweet deals to run my own weapons-manufacturing company to make whatever Peter invented. Who am I supposed to believe?"

She knew the feeling well. She felt like a Ping-Pong ball bouncing back and forth between trusting Colt and being convinced he was a bad guy who'd kidnapped her. She said reflectively, "I suppose at some point you just have to trust your gut."

He snorted. "My gut's so screwed up I barely know who I am, let alone who to trust."

They trudged on in silence after that.

Exactly when the cold crept inside her clothes and wrapped around her in a freezing blanket of misery, she didn't know. But gradually she realized her feet and hands had gone numb. And then she started stumbling more frequently. Her teeth started to chatter if she didn't consciously clench her teeth.

"You okay?" Colt asked.

"I'm f-f-f-fine."

Colt whipped around immediately and grabbed her hands. "Cripes, you're an ice cube. Count backward from ten to one for me."

She frowned. *What for?* But dutifully she started. "T-t-ten. N-n-nine." A pause. "Eight." A very long pause while she concentrated hard. "S-s-sev-v-v-ven." But then she got stuck. For the life of her she couldn't remember which number came next. She decided to try counting up from one to get to what came next. "Uhh…one. T-t-two—"

"That's enough. You're hypothermic. Bad guys on our tails or not, we've got to stop and get you warmed up. Now."

Warmth. It sounded like manna from heaven. She realized her teeth chattered uncontrollably, jaw clenching or not. Maybe that was what was giving her the sudden throbbing headache.

"Stay put. I've got to get you dry or you'll never warm up. I'm going to build a quick shelter, and then I'm getting you out of those wet clothes."

She retorted, "As l-lines g-go to g-get a g-girl out of her knickers, that's p-p-pretty l-l-lame."

He laughed quietly as he pulled out a knife nearly the length of her forearm and began slashing at branches on the trees around them. He spoke low over his shoulder. "Honey, if I wanted you out of your clothes, I wouldn't need to make up some line about you being hypothermic."

"Oh, y-y-yeah?"

"Yeah. Crouch down and wrap your arms around your middle. It'll help you conserve a little heat."

She was fairly certain she didn't have any heat left to conserve, but she played along. If it made him feel better, she'd curl up in this stupid fetal position. She asked, "Where are we going once we get out of these woods?"

"Good question. The feds no doubt have the cabin staked out by now. Although how they found the place, I haven't a clue. It's as if they had some sort of tracking device on us. But I'm sure I got rid of everything on the car."

She mentally gulped and felt the hard plastic of her cell phone in her pocket. She might know how they were being tracked. Earlier, she'd been hoping to be tracked, in fact. But by rescuers, not would-be attackers.

In just a few minutes Colt fashioned a long, low structure covered in broad overlapping leaves that neatly shed the rain.

"Your mansion awaits you," he announced with a flourish.

She dropped to her hands and knees and crawled inside. The interior was dark and green smelling, and the thick layer of boughs and leaves he'd laid for a floor was pokey. However, it did hold her up off the wet ground. He crawled in beside her and the space went from cozy to cramped. But heat immediately began to roll off his big body.

"Sheesh, you're better than a space heater."

"I've been working hard building this palace. If you're cold, come share the heat."

She huddled up against him, greedily soaking up all the warmth he cared to share with her. In a few minutes her teeth stopped chattering and the shivers cramping her muscles began to unwind.

Colt spoke quietly. "You want to tell me why I woke up alone in the cabin this afternoon?"

She sighed. Time to face the music. "You have to understand. All this has happened to me very fast. One day I'm developing film in my studio and living a nice, quiet life, and the next day this stranger I've never met before blows into my life. All of a sudden, people are chasing me and attacking me and I'm not sure I fully understand why. Then those men called me your hostage—" Her voice broke as the stress of the past day caught up with her all of a sudden.

"Ahh. And you believe them?" he asked quietly. "I suppose I can see that."

"Believed. Past tense. When they started shooting at me after you joined me, that was a pretty good indication you aren't the one trying to kill me."

His arms tightened around her. "I'm sorry I dragged you into this. Things weren't supposed to go to so bad. I swear I'll do everything in my power to keep you from getting hurt."

She released a slow breath. She believed him. She might even trust him. Which was a strange sensation. She'd learned long ago not to trust men in general—at least not with something personal and important like her heart or, oh, her life.

"While we're having true confessions," she said hesitantly, "I think I know how they found us. I went to the top of the mountain to get cell phone coverage and call for help."

He didn't go tense beneath her. In fact, if anything he relaxed. That was weird. But then he murmured in relief, "Mystery solved."

*Wow.* He wasn't going to yell at her? That was mature of him.

He asked, "So, did you get a hold of anyone?"

"No. I could never quite get coverage."

"Too bad. We could use some law-enforcement backup right about now."

"You're not mad at me?" she asked, surprised.

"No. It's my fault if I didn't inspire enough trust in you to believe me."

"But I led the bad guys straight to us."

He hugged her a little closer. "I'm just as at fault as you are. I didn't think about them tracking your cell phone signal. These guys are really good and I'm not operating at anything close to full capacity. We've got more important problems than pointing fingers at each other over who's responsible for them finding us."

"Speaking of which, what comes next?"

"Any revelations about jars while you were out here communing with nature?" he asked.

"No. Sorry."

"After we get some rest, we'll head for a road and see if we can flag someone down. And then we'll keep searching for the trigger."

"You are single-minded, aren't you?" she murmured.

"No. I'm fighting for my sanity."

# Chapter 6

She gulped. Not only did him losing his mind not bode well for her safety, but she worried about Colt personally. He was a decent man. An honorable one. It wasn't his fault he got captured and ended up in the same cell with Peter.

She spoke quietly. "Those men said they're from the government. Is that true?"

His jaw tightened. "Maybe. They seem to be trained a lot like me. If they are, they're a rogue group or flat-out spies. If we're lucky and we catch them, we may kill two birds with one stone. You and I would get left alone, and we could rid the government of them."

She frowned. "Is there more to this situation than you've told me? I feel like I'm missing something. What do you know that you're not telling me?"

He sighed. "You don't need to know that information."

"You want my help getting Peter out of your head? That's the price," she declared. "I want to know everything."

He exhaled long and hard. "Peter said you're a stubborn woman."

"Yeah, well, he no doubt thought you were a true blue hero, too. Clearly his judgment stunk."

Colt grinned unwillingly. "Good thing my career's already pretty much wrecked by my little psychiatric problem. My mission in Kyrgyzstan was to rescue Peter. And the reason I think it went to hell—the reason we failed and I ended up captured—is someone on our side sabotaged the mission."

"What are you saying?" she asked, shocked.

"I think someone inside the government wants to get whatever Peter was working on for himself or for whoever he is working for."

"Shouldn't you tell someone? Whoever it is that catches spies?"

"I did. They're the ones who told me I was crazy."

Appalled, she asked, "Do you think whoever sabotaged your rescue mission and those men chasing us work together?"

"Yes, I do."

"Did Peter know who they were?"

Colt stared at her, transfixed. "That's an excellent question."

She shrugged. "It would explain why he went to such great lengths to hide whatever it was he came up with. I think we both agree it must have been a weapon of some kind, yes? After all, Peter did work at a government weapons research facility."

Colt was very still. She could actually feel his brain processing information and seeking solutions. Finally, he said slowly, "If you're right and Peter knew the people who were after his work then and are sniffing around it now, that means the saboteurs and the guys chasing us now must have worked with Peter. Or at least whoever they're working for must have worked with Pete and been familiar with his work."

"Do you know who he worked with?"

Colt snorted. "Yeah. The jerks who've been calling me crazy."

"Well, that makes sense. They would need to discredit you so the government quits trying to extract whatever Peter hid in your head. Then they'd need to catch you and extract the secret themselves."

"They can try," Colt retorted grimly, "but I'll die before I reveal anything to them. My captors found that out the hard way in—" He broke off.

"What?" she breathed.

"It just occurred to me that my captors might have been working for the same person or persons as the men chasing me now do."

"If it's all related, what does that mean for us?"

"It means we have to be very, very careful. If these guys catch us, who knows what they'll do to us."

She gulped. She had no stomach for the kind of torture he'd endured during his captivity. Just witnessing one of his nightmares about it had shaken her to the core. No way could she withstand something like that.

"I'm scared," she whispered.

"Aww, honey. Don't be. I promise I'll keep you safe."

"But what if I don't feel safe?"

"Then I guess I'd just have to distract you."

That sounded interesting. "How would you do that?"

"I suppose I'd just wrap my arms more tightly around you—" he demonstrated, drawing her gently, but inexorably, closer "—and I'd breathe in the scent of your hair. Then I'd kiss your earlobe like this…" He nibbled his way down her neck, describing in half-whispered detail everything he was going to do next.

When he got to the part about slipping his hands under her shirt to feel the warmth of her skin and how her breasts would fill his cupped hands, how he'd knead them until she moaned and arched into him, she reached up reflexively to stop him. Except somehow, her hands ended up tangled in the collar of his shirt, her fingertips tracing the outline of his jaw, her entire body straining against his of its own free will.

He eased her shirt over her head, kissing his way across her collarbone to her bra strap. He lifted the thin satin with his teeth and pulled it aside, kissing a path of utter destruction in its wake. When the clasp popped open behind her back, she hardly noticed, so breathless was she at the way his tongue was swirling around the frantic peak of her breast through thin, damp fabric, his teeth grazing the sensitized flesh until she arched up off the ground, begging for more.

As she pressed against him, the clammy cold of his shirt contacted her skin. "Hey, you're falling behind," she teased. She stripped his shirt off quickly, baring his big, hard chest to her eager touch. Her pants magically peeled away from her legs and cold air hit her skin, jolting her. But then with a rattle of a buckle and a quick zip, his warm, naked legs twined with hers. Every part of him was solid. Muscular. Overwhelming. This was no lean, androgynous model. Colt was a man's man. A warrior. Vague alarm vibrated in the back of her head. He was not the kind of man she'd be able to manage easily. Okay, to manage at all.

"Has anyone ever told you you're intimidating?"

she mumbled against his chest. "Or that you kiss like a god?"

Smiling against her lips, he murmured, "A time or two." He deepened his kiss, inhaling her entire soul into him. When her head was spinning and she could barely form a thought, he added, "But none of my men could kiss me back like you do, honey."

Smiling, she pulled him down to her. "I hear marines are the best kissers."

"I'm no jarhead, in spite of Peter insisting on calling me one."

She laughed. "Peter said marines have the best stamina, too."

"Now those are fighting words, madam. Clearly, I'm going to have to uphold the honor of the United States infantrymen tonight." And then he kissed her so thoroughly she couldn't have answered even if she had been able to string words together into actual sentences in her scrambled brain.

Colt fought to control his raging need for this woman. Fought to hang on to his mind, holding off panic and hopelessness by sheer dint of will. Neither were impulses he'd ever given into before, not even during the worst of his captivity. Not even when Pete had died and he'd been so sure he was next—

A stunning thought hit him. He'd been rescued from his captors within a few days of Peter's death in a mission that had gone ridiculously smoothly. At the time he'd just been grateful to get out of hell alive. But for the first time he had to wonder about the timing of it all. He'd thought it horribly tragic that Peter had died just before help had come. But maybe help had come precisely because Peter had died.

If his captors had been in cahoots with a colleague of Peter's, and they'd been using Colt to get Peter to talk about his work, once Pete had died there would have been no point in holding Colt any longer. My God. Had that entire year of hell been an elaborate setup to trick Peter into revealing whatever he'd come up with?

Disbelief roared through Colt. He'd suffered agonies and insults to the human body that no mortal should ever be forced to endure. He'd comforted himself with the knowledge that he was serving his country. That he was doing the right thing. Being a hero. And it had all been *staged* to trick Peter?

Surely not.

But how could it *not* all be connected? Particularly after Colt got home and Peter's colleague, who'd been brought in to consult with Colt's shrinks, had been so adamant that Peter wasn't working on anything new or revolutionary. Come to think of it, that had also been the guy who first suggested Colt had a screw or two loose.

"Are you okay?" Layla asked hesitantly.

"Oh. Uh, yeah." Holy cow. Here he was nearly making love to a beautiful sexy woman, and he'd gone woolgathering like some senile old man!

To hell with spies and conspiracies and elaborate ruses. He was alive and free right now. With Layla. He had no idea if he'd be captured and mind-raped soon or not. But the two of them had this moment. And that was all he planned to think about.

He kissed her with all the desperation and passion he'd bottled up in his soul for the past year. It was a huge to relief to feel it rushing out of him in a violent torrent of need. And Layla, God bless her, absorbed every bit of it, taking everything into herself, smoothing out the raw edges and reflecting it back to him in a glorious display of reciprocated lust.

In fact, she'd gone so far as to become a bit of wild thing. Her nails scraped across his back, and the wordless, primal sounds she was making in the back of her throat exactly fit the earth beneath them and green leaves overhead. Thank God she didn't seem to need him to be civilized or suave tonight. He was too edgy, too ragged, to be the kind of cool intellectual she probably went for.

"What have you done to me, Colt?" she gasped.

He laughed shortly. "I think you're the one who's done something to me. I'm barely hanging on, here."

"You'd better keep up with me." She half laughed. "The reputation of the U.S. army rests on your shoulders." She ran her hands across those shoulders and shuddered with delight beneath him.

He half groaned. "I wouldn't want to let down the whole army and hundreds of years of proud tradition. Do me a favor. If the bad guys show up, punch them in the nose and tell them to get lost for me."

"I will." She grinned up at him in challenge and invitation.

He was no idiot. He didn't wait for the lady to ask twice. He groaned as he pressed into her tight heat, their bodies fitting together like puzzle pieces custom-cut for one another.

"Oh, my," she sighed in bliss.

"I believe there was some question about the strength of a U.S. army man?" he asked lightly. He surged powerfully within her, withdrawing and repeating the maneuver until she was rising up to meet his every thrust, moaning wordlessly and clinging to him as if she never planned to let go. He kept up the steady rhythm until she went taut beneath him, her entire body arching into a rictus of pleasure. She cried out as shudders wracked her from head to toe. She went limp and gazed up at him in something akin to awe. He knew the feeling. But the pride of the U.S. army wasn't served yet, no siree.

He resumed moving within her, barely containing the beast within. He ground out from between clenched teeth, "And then there was the question of the stamina of a U.S. army man."

Her eyes went wide and delighted as he stroked the fires within her to a higher pitch, yet. A need to explode began to build within him, but he held it in ferociously. To hell with the army. He wanted this to be epic for Layla.

She climaxed again, shattering around him so sweetly he almost lost it then and there. But he reached deep for all the reserved of self-discipline he'd learned in his sojourn through hell. He drove her to a third release. She'd have screamed on this one had he not kissed her deeply and drawn her cries directly into his lungs.

But still he forced himself to clutch at a tenuous thread of control. The way her internal muscles were clenching at him, coaxing him deeper into her, was driving him mad. He wanted to slam into her mindlessly, to let go of everything he was and pour it all into her. But he dared not. This was torture of the worst kind, for he imposed it upon himself. Exquisite pleasure beckoned just out of reach, and every fiber of his being begged him to allow himself the moment.

Must. Not. Must maintain control.

But then she climaxed a fourth time, keening with such intense pleasure, her muscles spasming around him with such power, her breasts pushing up at him with such rosy perfection that he lost the battle. He capitulated with a strangled shout of his own, his pent-up need bursting through with a violence that tore away all rational thought, leaving behind only the rawest, most primitive shreds of his identity.

Eventually, she murmured, "Maybe Valentine's Day isn't so bad after all."

He smiled and kissed her forehead tenderly. It was rapidly becoming his favorite holiday.

Long, blissful minutes passed before the soldier in him pushed forward, whispering at him of danger. His mind might know that to be true, but his heart didn't have the slightest interest in listening. Right now he wanted to collapse in the arms of his lover, to savor the way her breath caught unevenly, to kiss the bright spots of pleasure he'd put in her cheeks and to caress the warm flush over her entire body.

But the soldier shoved back, demanding that Colt pay attention. After all, Layla's safety was on the line, too. That tipped the scales.

He murmured, "We were supposed to rest in here and get warm, not to wear each other out. Unfortunately, my gut's telling me it's time to move on. When you've caught your breath let me know, and we'll continue."

Layla sighed. He knew the feeling all too well. "Okay," she mumbled gamely.

He smiled into her hair. He had to give her credit. She was tougher than she looked. She fished beneath herself for her underwear and twisted awkwardly putting it on. "I think the jarheads are going to have to concede this one to the army."

He opened his mouth to mumble an army oo-rah, but his sharp night vision caught her sudden frown, and he shut his mouth in alarm. Crap. He didn't want her getting any more bright ideas, like running off alone into the woods again. He needed a fast distraction tactic. He leaned over her and kissed her passionately, and bless her, she rose up to meet him with abandon.

Hell, she was pulling his attention away from the problem at hand a lot better than he was doing it to her. It was a struggle to roll away from her and reach for his pants. At least they were both plenty warm now. It was a wonder they hadn't set the forest around them on fire with all that burning passion.

*Focus, you idiot.*

He couldn't remember the last time he'd had so much trouble getting his head into the game. Bad men were out there in the night. And if they caught up with him and Layla, the bad men would probably kill her and kidnap him. He'd be killed, too, but not until they'd ripped Peter's secrets from his mind by whatever means necessary.

Raindrops pattered lightly on their leafy roof. The night's creatures were hunkered down avoiding the rain, so he couldn't count on nature's own perimeter alarm system. And then he heard a sound that made his blood run cold. It was distant. Muted. But that had definitely been a stick cracking.

He whispered urgently, "Finish getting dressed. Hurry."

Layla lurched against him. "Why?"

Civilians. They always asked why first before they did anything. A soldier jumped to follow orders first and asked why later. "Just do it. I'll explain later." *If there was a later for them.*

He reached for his shirt and dragged it on frantically. She reached for her clothes, finally catching his sense of urgency. They banged elbows and knees and got tangled up a time or two, but somehow they managed to get fully dressed remarkably quickly.

He pressed a finger to her lips, indicating that she

should be silent. She nodded, her eyes huge with fright. Smart girl. He eased out of the shelter, gesturing for her to follow.

He moved off cautiously through the trees. Although his night vision was fully adjusted, he still felt as blind as a newborn kitten. His pursuers would undoubtedly be wearing state-of-the-art infrared imaging night-vision goggles out here. Bastards. Stealth wouldn't work against their pursuers and their technology. His and Layla's only chance lay in getting away from here fast.

He took off running, opting to head downhill so Layla could keep up the breakneck pace for longer. Thankfully, the rain made the forest floor into a sodden, silent, mat that masked their racing progress.

They'd been running for perhaps a minute when, without warning, he heard a muffled pop and something hot and heavy slammed into his left side. He swore as fiery pain erupted in his ribs.

"What's wrong?" Layla gasped.

"Nothing." He wasn't about to tell her he'd been shot. She'd go hysterical on him for sure. All he could do was make himself and Layla the hardest possible targets they could be to the snipers behind them. He swerved to the right for ten seconds or so, and then leaped back to the left without warning. Had he not been hanging on tightly to Layla's arm, she'd have been separated from him for sure. He felt something warm and wet running down his left side and soaking his shirt. Grimly, he pressed onward.

Time stopped registering for him. It could've been a few minutes or it could've been an hour later when he staggered. Had Layla not yanked hard on his arm, he'd have gone down.

"Are you okay?" she panted.

"Gotta keep going," he grunted. But then he stumbled again. How much blood was he losing, anyway?

*He could almost hear Peter call him all kinds of a stupid fool from beyond the grave. And the twerp would be right, too. He was going to bleed to death, and then what good was he going to be to Layla?*

The world went black.

# Chapter 7

Layla couldn't help the soft cry of distress that escaped her throat when Colt stumbled and went down to his knees. He slumped for a moment, then shook his head and came back up to his feet, but something was terribly wrong with him.

"Talk to me," she urged in a panicked whisper that was more panting than words. "What's going on?"

"Bleeding out. Gotta stop it. Bind this wound before I die."

*Die? Bleed out? Oh, God.* They stopped in the shadow of a towering hemlock. "Where are you hurt? Lemme see," she demanded in a whisper.

Colt slid to the ground, leaning back against the tree trunk. He was holding his left side. Something black and oily-looking soaked his shirt. She wasted no time lifting his shirt. She gasped at the ugly, round wound in his side.

"What the hell happened to you?" she demanded. "When did you get shot?"

"Right after we left the shelter. I think the bullet's lodged against my rib. Didn't get to my lung. Feels like the rib's cracked, though. God, that hurts."

And coming from him that was saying something. Using adrenaline-jacked strength she didn't know she had, she ripped a strip off the bottom of his shirt and tied the makeshift bandage as tightly as she could around him. "Can we stop and rest a little while or are they still after us?"

"Don't know. Can't hear them right now."

"Can you move? I think we ought to keep going."

"Slave driver," he grumbled.

She was too scared to smile, but she appreciated his effort at humor as she hauled him to his feet. Once she got him vertical, though, he swayed unsteadily. "Put your arm around my shoulders and lean on me," she directed.

"We're not going to get far like this," he panted.

"It's better than nowhere at all. Unless you'd prefer to just sit down and wait for whoever's hunting us to find us and kill us."

"They won't kill me until they find out what I know."

"That's great for you," she snapped, "but I'm toast."

"Not if I refuse to talk until you're safe."

"You're assuming they won't shoot first and ask questions later. And given that you're sporting a bullet hole, I'd say that's a faulty assumption."

Color him impressed. That was actually an excellent piece of deductive reasoning. Of course, Peter had never called her stupid. Quite the opposite, in fact. And in his limited experience with her, Peter was right.

*Shut up and walk, Self.*

*Self* replied dryly that talking to *Self* was often a sign of delirium induced by excessive blood loss.

Yup, he was going crazy. Either that or dying.

Layla staggered a little under Colt's weight. It couldn't be a good sign that he was leaning on her so heavily. But he didn't complain of any discomfort as they stumbled down the mountain together. Every time the wind blew a flurry of water fell on them. It might not be raining at the moment, but they were still soaked in minutes.

She picked through ferns and downed trees and rocks hidden under dead leaves, just waiting to ambush and twist the nearest ankle. It was slow, difficult going. She had no idea what they were going to do when they reached the bottom of the mountain, but she would cross that bridge when they got to it.

About the same time as it started to rain again in earnest, she thought the steepness of the slope might be easing. She whispered to Colt, "I don't know where to go next. I only knew to go down."

He muttered between clenched teeth, "Survival rule of thumb is to follow rivers downstream. They always lead to human settlements."

Right. Downstream. Humans. Help. She tripped on a partially buried log and he gasped.

"I'm so sorry!" she exclaimed under her breath.

"Talk to me. Distract me."

She babbled under her breath, "I wish I had some painkillers for you, but unfortunately, I'm plumb out at the moment. The good news is I think we're almost to the valley floor. Maybe the going will be smoother when we get there."

In response his hand squeezed her shoulder weakly. Oh, Lord. He was slipping.

He grunted. "Look for a road. Flag down a car. Leave me. Go get help."

She jolted in dismay and whispered back angrily, "Are you kidding? No way am I leaving you. You're the one who knows what to do. Besides, I could never live with myself if I just left you. Not after what we've shared—"

The trees ended as abruptly as they had at the summit of the mountain. One moment they were in thick forest, the next they were at the edge of a meadow with cold rain slashing at their faces. The weeds bent over in uneven humps that made for rough going as they stumbled along the margin of the trees, paralleling the field.

"I feel sick," Colt muttered in chagrin. "I think I'm going to throw up."

"Go for it. Just point your head the other way, and don't stop walking."

"Head hurts…"

"When we get back to town and are safe, I promise I'll give you a whole bottle of aspirin. But we have to get there first. I know you don't feel good, but you have to keep going. For what it's worth, you're being very brave."

He didn't even snort in response.

"Stay with me, Colt," she said lowly. "I need you."

His voice was a bare sigh as he said, "Maybe I should just surrender to these guys."

She stopped, spinning fast to face him. "Don't you ever give up on me. You hear? I *need* you."

He gave her a crooked smile that was pure Colt and trailed his fingers down her cheek. She leaned her face into his palm, savoring his touch.

He murmured, "You need me, huh? I kinda like the sound of that. Don't know what I'd do without you, either. Only anchor to reality for me and all that."

Warmth spread through her as he looped his arm

resolutely around her shoulders and they resumed their painfully slow progress. She was his anchor? A big, strong guy like him needed her? She couldn't remember the last time anyone had truly needed her. Even Peter had eventually moved away and lived his own life. But Colt? *Cool.*

As they staggered onward Colt started to mumble randomly under his breath. A word here and there or a snippet of a sentence. Uh-oh. He was getting delirious. She had to get him to tell her what to do next before he went completely nonrational.

"How long should we keep walking?" she asked urgently.

"Water. Or road."

Okay then. She'd just keep heading down the valley until they came across one or the other.

"Laser. Solar mirror. Wipe out cities…hah. Kid stuff. Missiles knocked out of space…now that's impressive. Into right hands…"

Holy cow. Was his mental block breaking open in his delirium? Desperate to keep Colt with her and to hear anything he had to say about Peter's secret, she asked, "Did Peter design a weapon that can wipe out cities?"

A snort. "Missile killer."

Okay, what was the big deal about that? Why would something like that be so valuable that someone was going to all this trouble to get it? Aloud she asked, "Haven't we had patriot missiles for a long time?"

Another snort. "Prehistoric."

*O-kay.* "What's the big deal about a missile killer then?"

"No more nukes."

She pondered that for a moment before the full implications of it hit her between the eyes with the force of a sledgehammer. *No more nuclear weapons.* If Peter had designed a weapon system that could reliably pick a nuclear warhead out of space as it flew toward its target, then he might just have ended much of the threat of nuclear war for all mankind.

"Wow," she breathed. "Did Peter tell you that's what he invented?"

"Shh. Classified. Can't tell. Prison cell's bugged."

After that he fell mostly silent. Whether Colt was still delirious or not, she couldn't tell. And frankly, she didn't want to know. She took comfort in believing that he was lucid and would know what to do if some new crisis arose.

How long they walked along the edge of the valley, she had no idea. Long enough that her legs ached and her shoes felt like they were filled with lead.

And then, without warning, Colt stopped abruptly. She froze out of reflex. "Did you hear that?" he whispered.

"Hear what?"

"I think that was a car. Up ahead."

Abject relief flowed through her, releasing every bit of the dragging exhaustion she'd been holding at bay. They'd almost made it. Just a few more steps.

Colt's arm fell away from her and he eased forward cautiously. She followed wearily. He waved her down to a crouch and she peered ahead in the dark, seeing nothing. He glided forward a few more yards and that was when she spotted it. A bare strip of asphalt cutting across the meadow to a concrete bridge spanning a stream. They'd done it. They'd found both a road and water. Now. Which one to follow?

"I vote for the road," she muttered. The idea of walking along on nice, smooth pavement sounded like pure heaven.

"Agreed. We wait here for a car to come along," he replied. "You'll step out in the road to flag it down because a lone woman is a lot less threatening than a lone man. The driver's much more likely to stop for you than me."

"Wake me up when someone comes along, eh?" Her eyelids were suddenly so heavy she could barely hold them open. The adrenaline that had been sustaining her must've just given up the ghost.

Colt didn't look any better. He literally looked about ready to fall over. She looked up at the road and—

Her life flashed before her eyes as three dark, humanoid forms rose up out of the grass directly in front of her. They couldn't be more than thirty feet away.

Her entire being completely vapor locked. A single incongruous thought flashed through her shocked mind. She was going to *die* on Valentine's Day. Talk about a hex.

She clenched Colt's hand with all her strength and said in a normal speaking voice, "Uh, Colt? Someone's here."

His entire body jerked beside hers but he made no other move. Either he was incapable of it or thought discretion was the better part of valor at the moment. She squinted, trying to make our more details of the strangers. Oh, no. Every one of the men was pointing a rifle at them. And they didn't look like recreational hunters. Not with their faces painted black like that and wires running to their ears and to gadgets around their throats.

"Get up," one of the men snarled.

Colt tried to push up, but he collapsed right back down beside her. Not good. Apparently, he was done in. Which meant she was in charge of negotiations for the moment. Layla gulped. She had to think fast. Colt had been worried that she would be seen as expendable. She had to find a way—and soon—to convince these guys that they needed her alive.

"Who are you?" she demanded, praying she didn't sound nearly as scared as she was.

"Federal agents, ma'am."

"What agency? I'd like to see your badges, if you don't mind." Although she suspected their giant rifles were all the badges she was likely to see.

"That's need to know only," one of them retorted.

"Yeah, well, I need to know," she shot back. "If you expect me to talk without knowing who you are, you're sadly mistaken."

They looked at her in unanimous surprise. Didn't think she knew anything of value, did they? They were right, of course, but her life hung on convincing them otherwise. She glanced at Colt and declared, "I don't know about you, Colt, but I'm not saying another word until these jokers identify themselves."

Thankfully, he followed her lead. "Me neither. Mum's the word, boys."

A huddled conference followed. She watched closely for a moment to make a break for it, but one of the men always kept an eye on them. Given how weak Colt was, though, the two of them couldn't exactly out-sprint these guys through the woods. Not that she could outrun any commando on a good day. And this emphatically hadn't been a good day.

Except for their brief respite in the makeshift shelter. That had been spectacular. Colt made her feel more like a real woman than anyone ever had. Made her feel beautiful and powerful. He'd been amazing.

"Come with us," one of the men ordered brusquely.

"Where are we going?" she replied.

"We're the ones giving the orders," the guy retorted.

She planted her hands on her hips. "I happen to be a civilian, and I'm not obligated to take orders from anyone. Now, I want to see your badges and know who you are, or we're not moving from this spot. We'll wait for a car to come along and hitch a ride out of here."

Her mention of cars caused the men to glance nervously in both directions. Colt crossed his arms over his chest. "I'm with her. I'm not talking and I'm not walking until you guys cough up some ID."

Swearing under his breath, one of the men rolled his eyes and stepped forward, holding out an opened leather bifold wallet. "We're with the Defense Research Agency, for crying out loud."

She had no idea what the Defense Research Agency was, but she had learned one very important thing. These guys weren't prepared to kill her and Colt. At least not yet. She nodded stiffly and walked in the direction the nice man with the huge grin pointed.

One man led the way in front of them and the other two fell in behind. The odd little formation marched down the road toward a bend ahead. They'd almost reached it when, without warning, a sharp pain exploded in her neck. It felt like she'd been stung by a wasp.

"Oww!" she exclaimed. She reached up to bat it away and felt something hard and as long as her thumb sticking out of her neck. She looked over at Colt and saw what looked like a miniature dart sticking out of his neck, too.

Her knees start to buckle, and then everything went black.

## Chapter 8

Colt regained consciousness to the familiar feel of concrete beneath his cheek. He was an old pro at not opening his eyes, at continuing to fake being out cold. Anything to buy himself a few more minutes' reprieve from whatever his captors had in mind for him next. He relaxed on the floor, listening intently. Someone was breathing lightly nearby. It sounded like the person was at floor level. Layla, maybe?

One part of him hoped she was close for the comfort of her presence and so he could protect her. But another part of him—the part that had cold, hard experience with being a prisoner—wished desperately that she was nowhere near him right now. He wouldn't wish the things he'd been through as a prisoner on his worst enemy, let alone on a woman he cared about deeply.

When he heard no further movement nearby, he risked cracking one eye open a bit. The room was brightly lit, white on white and littered with computers and electronics at work stations scattered across the large space. It looked like a lab or research facility of some kind.

He checked automatically for hooks in the ceiling or walls that could be used to restrain a person. None. No drains in the floor for washing away blood, either. At least this room wasn't set up for torture. Not that a guy with a broomstick and a length of rope couldn't have him screaming like a woman in under five minutes, of course.

Peter's implanted memory tickled at the edges of his consciousness, probing, pushing. Oh, now that damned memory wanted to reveal itself! It had to wait until the one moment when Colt dared not remember the stupid thing to emerge? It figured. He chanted to himself, *Not yet, Pete. Not yet...*

Colt risked turning his head and spotted Layla lying on her side behind him. He swore under his breath. No wonder he wasn't tied up. Her presence changed everything. Their captors could use her to force him into cooperating, and both he and they knew full well it would work as a tactic. No way could he stand by and watch her suffer torture because he refused to talk. After all, he loved her.

The thought stopped him cold. Since when did he *love* Layla? In truth, he'd probably loved her at least a little before he ever met her in person. Peter had described her so vividly it was as if Colt had known her for years. She'd been the girl next door, the perfect woman he'd never had time to meet after he joined the army and started running all over the world. The best friend and confidante, loyal and kind and caring.

"Layla?" he whispered. "Are you awake?"

She shifted slightly, and her eyes half fluttered open.

She must just be coming out under the effect of the anesthesic. He tried again. "Layla. Wake up, honey."

She muttered, "Crud. It's not a dream. I was hoping it was."

He smiled crookedly. "Welcome to my nightmare."

"What are we going to do?" Panic was creeping into her voice, now. She was conscious enough to realize they were in a very bad situation. "I think maybe you're starting to remember. And the jar thing…I think I've figured it out. Peter liked to call you a jarhead, right? A jar without a lid?"

*Sonofagun.* She was right. The twerp had merely been saying that his secret was inside Colt's head. Then what was the damned trigger?

He said grimly, "The first thing we're going to do is remember we're in the driver's seat. We have the information they want. And if they mess with us too much, we'll refuse to give it to them altogether."

She lurched in alarm. "We can't give *any* of it to them! Peter's discovery could annihilate people as easily as missiles, right?"

Colt reached out and gathered her in his arms. "Don't say any more about that, sweetie. We could be monitored right now. Just be patient and stand your ground. It'll be all right. I promise."

"Promise?" she asked in a tiny voice.

"Cross my heart. Don't think about Peter. Don't mention him."

"A good idea in theory," she replied regretfully. "But that may not be possible."

"Why not?" he responded.

"I don't exactly have your iron self-control—"

A door opened behind him and she stopped speaking abruptly. Which was just as well.

"I see our guests are awake," a male voice said pleasantly. "Excellent. It's time to end this little game of cat and mouse."

Colt looked up at the speaker, a gray-haired man who appeared to be in his late fifties. The hired muscle, in the form of four thugs, stood behind him. "And you would be who exactly?" Colt asked.

"I'm the person to whom you're going to tell everything," the man replied confidently.

Colt snorted. Him and what army? None of these men had the same eager look in their eyes that Khan got at the prospect of causing pain. And shy of Khan, not too many people in the world could get to him.

"Boys." The man gestured and two men stepped forward to hoist him to his feet. He gave Layla a quick squeeze and let her go as the thugs ripped him out of her arms. Colt didn't look down at her. He didn't dare show any weakness where she was concerned.

"Over here." Gray-hair moved to stand by an elaborate computer with multiple monitors and a large electronic drawing pad beside it.

Colt was shoved onto the stool before the setup.

"Okay, McQuade. I've gone to a lot of trouble to get my hands on you. Time to cough up the big invention Peter Morrison came up with while he was in prison with you."

"What makes you think I have any idea what he cooked up in prison?"

"You two were crammed together in a little box for nearly a year and you expect me to believe he didn't share it with you?" Gray-hair snorted.

Colt shrugged. "Sorry to disappoint you, buddy. But he didn't tell me a thing. Peter could keep a secret."

"Bring the girl over here," Gray-hair directed.

Colt's jaw tensed. "If you mess with her, I guarantee you will never get a thing out of me. I'll take whatever I know straight to hell with me."

"You don't want to see her pretty little face wrecked, do you?"

"Look. I just met her. She wanted to know what happened to her old friend Peter. She doesn't know anything."

"You've been with her around the clock. You expect me to believe she knows nothing?"

Colt answered casually, "Clingy female. Not my type if I do say so myself." He dared not glance at Layla to soften his words in any way. These bastards *had* to believe she meant nothing to him.

"Guess we'll have to jog your memory a bit, then," Gray-hair announced.

Relief rolled through Colt. A little old-fashioned beating was something he knew exactly how to handle. Weird how comfortable it was. The old routine once more. Except this time, he had to find a way to hold off Peter's damned memory implant.

The fist to his left eye caught him off guard. His head snapped and he let it, absorbing as much of the power of the blow as he could with his head and neck. He'd give the sucker punch a B– for pain, but a solid B+ for surprising him. Another blow, this time to his jaw. *Better power, but lousy aim.*

As the second man joined the first in using him as a punching bag, it became harder and harder not to reach for Peter's memory. It was the key to making the pain stop. He must stay strong. For Layla. For his country. Protect Peter's secret. Hell, Peter had died protecting it. The least he could do was take a beating in the name of protecting Peter's discovery.

But then a strangled cry from behind him had him twisting on his stool in spite of himself. A whale of a right cross took his exposed cheek by surprise. *Layla*. Was she okay?

Her fist was all but stuffed into her mouth as tears streamed down her face. "They hur'ing you?" he croaked around his split and swollen lips.

"Oh, God, Colt. Don't let them do this to you." She was untouched. They were apparently satisfied to make her watch.

He shrugged, ignoring the stabbing pain from a couple of cracked ribs that the movement cost him. "I'll live un'il these jokers figure ou' we don' know where Pe'er hid his secre'."

"Guess we'll just have to do this the hard way then, won't we, McQuade?" the gray-haired man snarled. "Go get the stuff."

One of his henchmen left and came back in a minute with a car battery, a pair of jumper cables, a pair of sponges and a bucket, presumably full of water. Reflexive horror rippled through Colt's body. Funny how his nerves remembered even when his conscious mind did not.

He must take this torture. Let it roll over him and through him and believe that when it was over he would still exist. It was all about simple survival now.

Terror shivered through Colt. In retrospect, he'd taken much more of Khan's abuse than he could believe. But everyone had a breaking point. Hell, he'd broken. The day had come when he'd been willing to tell Khan anything the bastard wanted to know. The only saving grace had been that he didn't have the information Khan wanted. He didn't know what Peter's work had been about.

He wasn't proud of it, but the day had come when he'd begged Peter to tell him what he'd invented. But Peter had steadfastly refused. He might have been a civilian, might not have been much of a physical specimen. But the man had a will of steel. He'd never once wavered. Never once given in to Colt's pleading. Not Peter. The guy had been a hero in every sense of the word.

He owed Peter one last heroic stand of his own. No matter if he was shot. No matter if the woman he loved was distraught. He *had* to stay strong. For Peter *and* Layla.

In the weeks immediately following his release, he'd gone through endless survivor's guilt attacks, reliving every single time he'd broken under Khan's torture. He'd wished each of those moments back. Wished he'd had a chance at a do-over. Wished he'd held out just a little bit longer. Apparently, his wish had come true.

He would prevail this time. If nothing else, this time he would prove to himself that he wasn't weak or a coward. He would be the hero Layla thought he was. Ahh, God, Layla. Dreams of her—her portrait painted vividly in his mind by Peter even before he'd met her—had sustained him for so long he barely knew where his dreams ended and the reality of her began. Peter had loved her. So he'd loved her. The two jumbled together in his head.

Gray-hair and his boys continued their dastardly work and he fell into a detached state where his brain and body disconnected from one another. He watched from a distance as they abused his body, causing it horrendous pain. He noted that this bunch wasn't half-bad at their work. They weren't damaging him so seriously that he'd be too broken to continue torturing for a good long time.

But then something odd happened. His memories of Khan's torture and his current experience began to run together in his head, past blurring with present, forgotten tidbits of before surfacing and mingling with disjointed details from now.

He struggled frantically to hold the two apart. He wasn't sure why he had to, but he was sure it was the right thing to do. He was failing. Failing like he'd failed before, breaking under the strain of the physical agony. Giving way. Slipping…

The shroud hanging between his awareness and Peter's implanted memory tore away all in a rush. He almost heard a rending noise in his brain as the mental barrier holding back Peter's memories shredded apart. No longer was he divided in two. Only he remained. Raw. Naked. Weak. And dammit, he remembered exactly what Peter had planted in his brain!

Withstanding what Gray-hair and company were doing to him had just become immeasurably harder. Now he held in his hands the means to stop the torture by giving in and giving them what they wanted.

Dammit, he was supposed to be the tough one! The hardcore soldier. The one who could take anything and endure. But in the end Peter was the one who'd had the strength to take it. The strength to say no to Colt when he'd begged to know the secret. Enough strength for both of them.

And now it was his turn to be strong for both of them. His turn to be the guardian of the secret. So be it.

A distant voice threatened him. Told someone to hook up the battery. Cut his shirt off. Colt barely noticed. As memories tied up with the secret came pouring back, he suddenly remembered the night Peter had hypnotized him. His cell mate had been sick and badly injured. Pete had known somehow that he wasn't going to live much longer. He'd asked a last favor of his friend, and Colt had not been able to turn down the last wish of a dying man.

How could he? Peter had been so indomitable for so long, had been Colt's rock through hell and back. He'd owed it to the guy.

That had been the night Peter hypnotized him. The night Peter planted memory of the design for the ultimate missile killer system in Colt's head and then hid it so carefully.

Peter had beaten Khan at his own game. Only Peter's body had eventually broken. But never his mind. Never that which had made him Peter.

He could do the same, dammit.

Colt chanted to himself, *I am Colt. I will endure. I will hang on for Layla. I will turn my weakness into my strength. They think they're hurting me by torturing me in front of her. But I will draw comfort and inspiration from her presence.* A vision of her radiant smile and shining blue eyes swam in his mind's eye. She was his own personal angel. And if he had anything to say about it, he was never going to let go of her for as long as he lived. Now *that* was something worth hanging on for.

Something cold and wet slapped against his chest. He remembered the sound and sight of Layla's pleasure ringing in his ears. He smiled. A jolt of agony seared through him, like a lightning bolt had just struck him. It shocked him out of his memories. But it didn't erase her face. He'd done it. He'd found the key. A beautiful, stubborn, funny woman who maybe loved him a little.

His eyes opened. He was at peace. A bright white room loomed before him. Layla sobbed somewhere behind him. An evil bastard with gray hair scowled, torturing him for information he would never, ever reveal. And none of it mattered. He had Layla in his heart.

Layla had had enough. She surged forward, slamming into the guy with the jumper cables from behind. He fell forward, landing on the instruments of Colt's torture and giving a thoroughly satisfying scream as he got a hefty dose of his own medicine. She spun, snarling, and leaped for the next man. She was prepared to rip his eyeballs out bare-handed. They'd attacked her man, *her Colt,* and she was out for blood, now.

The thug threw up his arms, swearing violently, to ward her off.

It took all three of the remaining thugs to subdue her, and all of them sported bloody scratches and were swearing freely before they finally pinned her arms at her sides.

Gray-hair stepped close. "You want a taste of the battery, bitch?" he growled.

"Leave her alone!" a strident voice declared from at her feet.

*Oh, Lord, no.* Her stomach dropped violently. Colt mustn't give up Peter's secrets. Millions...billions...of lives rode on him not talking.

Colt spoke calmly. "Get your goons off Layla and I'll give you what you want."

Gray-hair gestured at the computer station. "You first, Captain McQuade."

"No!" Layla wailed as Colt climbed painfully to his feet and sat down in front of the computer. *God, no. She wasn't worth it!* "Stop!"

But he picked up an electronic stylus and commenced sketching rapidly. It didn't take long before Colt announced, "You'll forgive the roughness of the sketch. This is the first time I've actually written it down. I believe your scientists will get the idea, however."

Gray-hair examined the intricate drawing closely. Layla couldn't make heads nor tails of it, but then, she was no engineer. A printer across the room spit out a copy of

Colt's drawing. One of the thugs let go of her arm and moved over to retrieve it. He showed it to Gary-hair, who nodded tersely.

"Thank you for your cooperation, Captain McQuade."

Colt replied tiredly, "Go to hell."

And just like that, Gray-hair and his associates had let her go and swept out of the room. She rushed forward and wrapped her arms around Colt as he swayed on the stool.

"Are you crazy?" she cried. "How could you have done that?"

He straightened in her arms all of a sudden, abruptly much stronger and more alert than he'd been when the thugs were in the room. "That was quite some display of mama-bear rage, Layla," he murmured in amusement. "Very convincing. Couldn't have fooled them without you."

Fooled them? What the heck was he talking about? "I beg your pardon?" she demanded. "You mean you put me through hell like that and it was an *act?* I thought they were killing you!"

He grinned. "Oh, they made a good faith effort to mess me up. Succeeded to some degree, too. But I wasn't about to die with the rest of my life with you in it waiting for me."

"The rest—" she started.

The door burst open and a half-dozen armed men in military uniforms burst into the room. She started violently, flinging herself protectively in front of Colt as best she could. Apparently, she wasn't quite done playing mama bear, yet.

"We're the good guys, ma'am," one of them announced in alarm.

Like she could tell the difference from the good guys and the bad guys at this point? She harrumphed, unimpressed.

Someone called out, "Captain McQuade, tell her."

An amused voice came from behind her. "These are my guys, Layla. They work for me. I trust them completely. Did you catch that bastard and his minions?"

"Yes, sir. We apprehended your captor and his men in the hall before we came in here. They never knew what hit them. A few of the guys are loading them in one of our vans and taking them in for questioning now."

Layla's jaw dropped. "How did this happen? Are you sure you can trust these men, Colt? I thought you said someone sabotaged the mission—"

He put an arm around her waist and drew her close. "Sabotaged it from the outside, honey. Not from within my unit. These guys nearly died trying to save me and keep me from getting captured."

One of them piped up, "He's telling the truth. We fought like hell to go back and get him. He was the one who ordered us to leave him and save ourselves."

Colt spoke up mildly, "Sweetheart, if you wouldn't mind putting away your claws for a few minutes, I could use a little medical attention. I wouldn't say no to a spot of morphine right about now."

She spun, concerned. Who knew she had all these raging maternal instincts? Maybe she was cut out to have kids after all. And if Colt meant what he'd said about having her in the rest of his life...

Two soldiers rushed forward and shouldered her aside to examine Colt.

Before she hardly knew what had hit her, she and Colt had been whisked out of what turned out to be a big brick building and into a large step van. At least twenty more men in military uniforms milled around outside. A big cheer went up when she and Colt emerged from the building. Colt grinned and waved at them.

"Where are we going?" she murmured to him as the two of them were loaded into a step van.

"There's a military hospital not too far from here. I imagine that's where they're taking us. They'll treat my injuries and make sure you're not dehydrated or in shock."

"I may be shocked, but I'm not in shock," she declared stoutly. Although it took a few minutes bumping down a road in the van for her really accept that they were safe. Alive. Nightmare over.

It took a few minutes more for her adrenaline level to drop enough for her to begin thinking even close to logically again. And as soon as she did, her first question to McQuade's men was, "How did you guys find us?"

One of them laughed. "You, ma'am."

"Excuse me?" She blinked at the soldier in surprise.

"We've been, umm, keeping an eye on the captain for the past few weeks. He said someone was trying to kill him and we believed him. When some of our superiors seemed inclined to blow off his claims, it turned out a bunch of the guys in our unit had family emergencies of one kind or another and we all ended up on leave."

Colt piped up from the stretcher he was lying on in the middle of the van, "And what? You followed me?"

"As much as we could. With all due respect, sir, you're pretty hard to keep tabs on when you don't want to be found."

Grins passed around the van and another soldier took up the tale. "You seemed to get spooked about a week ago and we lost you when you went to ground. But then a Valentine's card appeared in your mailbox waiting to be mailed. We read the address and staked out the place." He nodded at Layla. "Your apartment, ma'am. Sure enough, sir, you showed up there a couple of nights ago and we had your trail again."

Colt swore softly. "Amateur mistake to use my own mailbox."

One of the other men added, "Good thing you did. Only way we found you. That Valentine's card was a lucky break for us."

Layla smiled at Colt. That card was turning out to be lucky in more ways than Colt's men knew. He smiled back at her, and then said, "Continue. How did you men find us today?"

"Well," the first one said, "not only did you two show up at her place a few nights ago, but those thugs who were after you did, too."

Layla interrupted, "Who are they, anyway?"

"The ringleader used to work for the Defense Research Agency. He got fired a while back and went into business trying to steal American military research secrets. He used what he knew from before he left the agency to track down various important researchers and bribe or blackmail them into selling him information. The he sold it to the highest bidder on the black market."

Layla reached out to hold Colt's hand. "So why did this guy go after Colt?"

Colt himself answered that one. "Not me. Peter."

The men around them nodded. "Anyway," one of them continued, "we were just going to follow you two, but then that information broker got onto your trail. So, we tailed him."

One of the other men laughed. "Yeah, and he was a hell of a lot easier to follow than you two. He left a trail a mile wide." The guy shrugged. "He seemed to lose you yesterday. But then all of a sudden yesterday afternoon he went crazy and made a beeline for some mountain in the middle of nowhere. We tagged along, and when he captured you two, we moved in for the kill."

"You could've busted in a little sooner," Layla griped.

Colt squeezed her hand. "It's not as easy as it looks to barge in and rescue hostages. Particularly if you want those hostages to live. We're alive and that bastard is in custody. It all worked out okay."

The soldiers laughed. "It helped when your girl went crazy. She provided just the distraction we needed to pull the attention of the lookouts away from the approaches to your location. Once they were all watching her go crazy and trying to subdue her, we were able to move in."

Layla stared at the fellow in blank disbelief. She'd helped rescue them? Seriously? Warmth started to spread inside her. Well, all right, then.

She frowned down at Colt lying on the ambulance cot. "Why did you give them Peter's design?"

He grinned up at her. "I didn't. Peter explained to me once how a microwave oven works, so I drew a schematic of that. With as many embellishments as I could think of to make it look complicated."

"For real? But what if they'd realized what you'd done? Wouldn't they have killed you? Wasn't that a heck of a risk to take?"

He laughed. "You must be getting back to your usual self. You're firing forty-two questions at a time at me again."

She made a face at him. "What about the real design, then?"

He tapped his head. "All in here. As soon as I get access

to another computer-design system, I should be able to sketch it out for the real Defense Research Agency."

"Then it's truly over?" she asked.

He looked at her in quick concern. "The mission's over, yes. But hopefully not us."

She smiled brilliantly at him. He hadn't been kidding when he'd made that comment about the rest of his life with her? *Cool.*

He wrapped his arms around her and pulled her down to him. He scooted over a little in the bed and she stretched out beside him. She felt a little weird cuddling in front of his men, but if he didn't mind, she didn't, either. It was a tight fit on the narrow cot, but she didn't plan on being more than a few inches away from him for some time to come anyway. They lay together in silence for a few minutes while she reflected on the past few days.

Finally, she said, "Do you remember what today is?"

"Sunday?"

"No. Valentine's Day!"

He commented casually, "Hmm. Interesting." A pause. "Did you know that more men propose to their girlfriends on Valentine's Day than on any other day of the year by a factor of ten?"

Her heart bumped hard against her ribs. "Is that so? I never knew."

"The way I heard it from Pete, you never really got into the spirit of the Valentine's Day much, though."

"I never had anyone to get into the spirit of it with," she retorted.

"Ahh. So there might be hope for me convincing you it's a worthy holiday?" he asked.

"What did you have in mind?"

He shifted and slid out from underneath her. She sat up in alarm. A couple of grinning soldiers slid over to make room for him and he knelt on the floor of the van in front of her.

"Layla, I feel like I've known you forever. Meeting you in person confirmed everything I already knew about you from Pete. He always said you and I would make a perfect couple, and I have to agree with him. You have been my anchor and my sanity. You have saved my life and saved my soul. Will you do me the very great honor of considering becoming my wife?"

Okay, that was the most romantic thing anyone had ever said in the history of the world—at least that anyone had ever said to her. A smile spread through her heart and across her face, so big and wide she could barely contain it.

"No—" she started.

A collective indrawn breath echoed sharply against the metal van walls.

She continued on, "I won't just consider it, Colt. Of course I'll marry you!"

He wrapped her in his arms and kissed her thoroughly while his men cheered around them. Beneath the din, he murmured to her, "I am crazy, you know. Crazy about you."

"Do you realize that next year I'm going to have to hex you and me at our annual Valentine's dinner?"

He chuckled. "Sounds like a new tradition. Pete would approve."

And so he would have. Funny how across time and even the veil of death itself, Peter had managed to bring the two of them together. That had been some Valentine's card, indeed.

\* \* \* \* \*

# COMING NEXT MONTH

## Available February 22, 2011

ROMANTIC SUSPENSE

SRSCNM0211

# REQUEST YOUR FREE BOOKS!

2 FREE NOVELS
PLUS
2 FREE GIFTS!

### ▼ Silhouette®
# ROMANTIC
## SUSPENSE
*Sparked by Danger, Fueled by Passion.*

SRS11

USA TODAY *bestselling author Lynne Graham*
*is back with a thrilling new trilogy*
SECRETLY PREGNANT, CONVENIENTLY WED

*Three heroines must marry alpha males to keep*
*their dreams…but Alejandro, Angelo and Cesario*
*are not about to be tamed!*

*Book 1—JEMIMA'S SECRET*
*Available March 2011 from Harlequin Presents®.*

JEMIMA yanked open a drawer in the sideboard to find
Alfie's birth certificate. Her son was her husband's child.
It was a question of telling the truth whether she liked it or
not. She extended the certificate to Alejandro.

"This has to be nonsense," Alejandro asserted.

"Well, if you can find some other way of explaining how
I managed to give birth by that date and Alfie not be yours,
I'd like to hear it," Jemima challenged.

Alejandro glanced up, golden eyes bright as blades and
as dangerous. "All this proves is that you must still have
been pregnant when you walked out on our marriage. It
does not automatically follow that the child is mine."

"'I know it doesn't suit you to hear this news now and I
really didn't want to tell you. But I can't lie to you about it.
Someday Alfie may want to look you up and get acquainted."

"If what you have just told me is the truth, if that little
boy does prove to be mine, it was vindictive and extremely
selfish of you to leave me in ignorance!"

Jemima paled. "When I left you, I had no idea that I was
still pregnant."

"Two years is a long period of time, yet you made no
attempt to inform me that I might be a father. I will want
DNA tests to confirm your claim before I make any deci-

sion about what I want to do."

"Do as you like," she told him curtly. "*I* know who Alfie's father is and there has never been any doubt of his identity."

"I will make arrangements for the tests to be carried out and I will see you again when the result is available," Alejandro drawled with lashings of dark Spanish masculine reserve.

"I'll contact a solicitor and start the divorce," Jemima proffered in turn.

Alejandro's eyes narrowed in a piercing scrutiny that made her uncomfortable. "It would be foolish to do anything before we have that DNA result."

"I disagree," Jemima flashed back. "I should have applied for a divorce the minute I left you!"

Alejandro quirked an ebony brow. "And why didn't you?"

Jemima dealt him a fulminating glance but said nothing, merely moving past him to open her front door in a blunt invitation for him to leave.

"I'll be in touch," he delivered on the doorstep.

*What is Alejandro's next move? Perhaps rekindling their marriage is the only solution! But will Jemima agree?*

*Find out in Lynne Graham's*
*exciting new romance*
*JEMIMA'S SECRET*

*Available March 2011*
*from Harlequin Presents®.*

# Start your Best Body today with these top 3 nutrition tips!

1. **SHOP THE PERIMETER OF THE GROCERY STORE:** The good stuff—fruits, veggies, lean proteins and dairy—always line the outer edges of the store. When you veer into the center aisles, you enter the temptation zone, where the unhealthy foods live.

2. **WATCH PORTION SIZES:** Most portion sizes in restaurants are nearly twice the size of a true serving and at home, it's easy to "clean your plate." Use these easy serving guidelines:
   - Protein: the palm of your hand
   - Grains or Fruit: a cup of your hand
   - Veggies: the palm of two open hands

3. **USE THE RAINBOW RULE FOR PRODUCE:** Your produce drawers should be filled with every color of fruits and vegetables. The greater the variety, the more vitamins and other nutrients you add to your diet.

Find these and many more helpful tips in

## YOUR BEST BODY NOW
by
# TOSCA RENO
WITH STACY BAKER

Bestselling Author of
**THE EAT-CLEAN DIET®**

*Available wherever books are sold!*

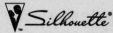

# ROMANTIC
## SUSPENSE
### *Sparked by Danger, Fueled by Passion.*

# CARLA CASSIDY
## *Special Agent's Surrender*

There's a killer on the loose in Black Rock,
and former FBI agent Jacob Grayson isn't about
to let Layla West become the next victim.

While she's hiding at the family ranch under Jacob's
protection, the desire between them burns hot.
But when the investigation turns personal,
their love and Layla's life are put on the line,
and the stakes have never been higher.

**A brand-new tale of the**

# LAWMEN
## *of* BLACK ROCK

*Available in March wherever books are sold!*

**Visit Silhouette Books at www.eHarlequin.com**

SRS27718

HARLEQUIN®
*Super Romance*®

Top *author*
# Janice Kay Johnson

*brings readers a riveting new romance*
*with*

# Bone Deep

Kathryn Riley is the prime suspect in
the case of her husband's disappearance
four years ago—that is, until someone tries
to make her disappear…forever. Now
handsome police chief Grant Haller must
stop suspecting Kathryn and instead begin
to protect her. But can Grant put aside the
growing feelings for Kathryn long enough
to catch the real criminal?

## Find out in March.

*Available wherever*
*books are sold.*